SNAP-SHOT ARTIST

"Hang if you want to," Haines said. "But if it was me, I wouldn't hang at all. I'd settle up with Freeman without going to all the trouble you're going to."

"Ain't no trouble," Keeley said, lovingly filing the *sear* off his new Colt—the first requirement of the snap-shot artist.

"Wake up!" Haines said harshly. "Guns are pretty, but an accident will beat one every time. And a hard-rock mine like the *Sweet Betsy* is murder for accidents."

Keeley set the gun down carefully and leaned toward the mine owner. "What kinda accident did you have in mind?"

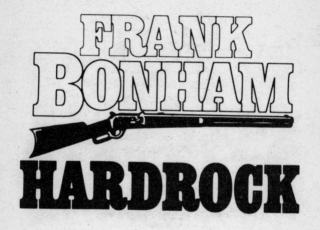

FRANK BONHAM

HARDROCK

BERKLEY BOOKS, NEW YORK

HARDROCK

A Berkley Book / published by arrangement with
the author

PRINTING HISTORY
Dell Edition / 1958
Berkley edition / July 1979
Second printing / October 1981

ISBN: 0-425-05068-8

A BERKLEY BOOK ® TM 757,375
PRINTED IN THE UNITED STATES OF AMERICA

1

THE FIRE WAS BURNING in the bottom of a gully, hidden by sheets of rusty iron which let only a few sparks of light burn through. You would hardly notice it, thought Drusilla Croft, gazing down from the lookout on the dark slope, unless you knew it was there. Above her on a ridge were the coffinlike structures of an old stamp-mill. On the hillsides stood the skeletons of old gallows-frames. Faintly she heard a gusty flapping, as her father pumped the bellows which kept the refining furnace at smelting temperature.

All summer they had been reworking the old mine tailings without detection. Nor was there reason to believe they were being watched tonight. Nevertheless she was uneasy. She had dreamed of a black dog last night, a sure omen of trouble; and today an uneasy mood had teased her—just a woman-mood, perhaps, a woman-sense quivering like the antennae of a butterfly because long ago, perhaps, something disastrous had happened here.

Mine women had those senses, and it was reckless to ignore them. The day before her father lost his leg in an accident, her mother had broken two needles; but he had gone down in the cage the next day anyway. And the cable had broken. And now Bill Croft was good only for a little work like cobbing out the bad rock when the mines were operating.

But this year of falling silver prices most of the mines were not operating, so that poaching at deserted stamp-mills was all that was left to him.

Certainly poaching was no great crime, the girl thought indignantly. A hardrock man whose strength was buried in the mines ought to have first peck at the tiny grains of gold the earlier birds had missed. But last spring a big, self-assured young man named Shepley Freeman had leased all the tailings in the area and had posted *Keep Out* signs. So they had to start working by night.

Suddenly from the mill buildings there was a sharp rasp of metal. Turning quickly, the girl peered up the dark slope. Behind the eyeless windows there was no light. Above the corrugated-iron roofs the stars glittered like diamonds in black ink. Could have been an owl on the roof, she thought. Then she heard it again: the rusty squawk of a hinge.

Quickly she tossed a warning pebble down the slope. At once the panting of the bellows ceased. Rising, she placed her hands on her hips and studied the mill. A tall, slender girl, she had the fair hair and golden look of girls who spent much time in the open. *"Brush your hair as if it was gold,"* her mother used to admonish her, *"for it's the only gold a mine girl will ever have."* When she moved it was with the grace of an Indian girl carrying a water-jug on her shoulder.

Now a shadow detached itself suddenly from the buildings, and a man came striding down the path between the old wooden tanks. In the sallow moonlight, she recognized the long-legged stride and the tall frame with the neat, flexible taper of an ax-handle: Shepley Freeman! Quickly Drusilla threw a second warning stone. Pulling her skirts knee-high she started down the hill, running lightly with her blond braids tossing. From the bottom she'd work west across the next ridge and descend practically into her back yard in the ghost town of Hornitos. But now Freeman was running too, coins and keys jingling as his boots thudded behind her.

"No use running, Drusilla!" he called impatiently.

No use, eh? she thought. In her moccasins, she could outrun any man afoot. But because of her father, who could not run at all, she slowed a bit to trick Freeman into following her while Bill Croft lost himself among the old structures and tangled mesquite trees.

But of course the gold had to be left. Such rotten luck! she thought angrily. To work all week hammering and grinding, and have him walk in just as the little thimble of metal settled out in the crucible! The unfairness of it! For there were more tailings in his lease than Freeman could sift in ten years, with his homemade furnace and salvaged equipment.

And the real pity of it was that for a month, now, he had not even worked them, and would probably never work them again. For he'd had the luck to blunder upon a very nice silver claim last month. Dru and her father had watched the geologists and engineers sink their test shafts, perform their solemn head-scratching, and trudge off to advise Tom Haines, Freeman's landlord on the Hornitos tailings, to buy a half interest in the claim.

Naturally Freeman hadn't told them about his good luck. But Haines had hired Bill Croft, as a man who knew the local formations better than anyone, to go over the prospects before he signed with Freeman. After all the book-miners had had their say, he had come to an old hardrock man for the final word. They said he'd been a gambler before he came to Arizona. Maybe it was true, for it was like a gambler to ask the blessing of a Cousin Jack before he made a bet as big as this one.

Bill Croft could have killed the whole thing, no doubt, just by shaking his head. But he had told Haines, "Go ahead. It's a good one." A good one was what Tom Haines needed, with all his other mines dying of the poor-ore disease.

Yet it never occurred to Shepley Freeman to take down his *Keep Out* signs as a gesture of gratitude. Instead, here he was at night, stalking his benefactor like a hunter!

As Dru ran lightly and almost silently, a voice with the power of a shotgun came from down the hill: "As you were, Croft! Save me the cost of a bullet!"

Drusilla faltered, angry and humiliated. For she knew that voice, too: the man closing in on her father was Charlie

Dennis, Tom Haines's superintendent. So Freeman had dragged Dennis in to help him discipline a one-legged miner and a girl!

Sheet-metal grated as her father sought to hide the equipment. Then something went wrong: the furnace-cover clattered on the ground, and a morsel of light, hot as a star-fragment, burned a hole in the darkness. Bill Croft was revealed lifting a crucible with a pair of tongs. A few rods down the gully the mine-boss was striding after him with a short-barreled rifle in his hands. Croft dropped the crucible and hurried at his peg-legged trot up the gully. Dennis halted and threw the carbine to his shoulder. Drusilla screamed.

Above her, Freeman bawled: "Hold it, Dennis! No foolishness!" A snake's-tongue of flame lashed from the rifle, the gunshot crashing and reverberating through the hills. Splinters flew as Croft's wooden leg disappeared. Sprawling full length, he drew his legs up and waited. Dennis swiveled the loading lever. Then, changing his mind, he lowered the gun and strode after the miner.

Dru started down the hill again, but her foot turned on a loose stone. She stumbled and landed flat. An instant later Freeman was upon her. She sat up, dazed and dusty. Then she clenched her fists, her eyes furious.

All right, young fellow! she thought fiercely, as he leaned over her, *I'll give your ungrateful hide the tongue-lashing it's been needing!*

2

ALL SUMMER SHEPLEY FREEMAN had suspected that the Crofts were poaching on his lease. He had the concentrates from two other mills to work, however, and knowing the Crofts needed the money he hadn't bothered them. Besides, there had turned out to be little profit in working the old concentrates. Rent and materials had leached away his small investment far more greedily than his chemicals went after the gold and silver in the tanks.

But yesterday Charlie Dennis had questioned him in Travertine, the sunbaked supply center down on the desert, about whether any work was going on at Mill Number Three. So at last Shepley knew he had to put an end to the Crofts' petty thievery, for his lease required him to pay rent plus a percentage of his refinings. It was that lost percentage that was on Dennis's mind.

Shepley found the girl huddled on the slope. Down the hill big Charlie Dennis was mauling Croft like a terrier he had trapped in his hen-house. Shepley's mouth tightened in anger; but for the moment it was Dennis's show.

"Are you hurt?" he asked the girl.

"I feel fine!" she said in an angry gasp. "Did you have to bring Dennis? Couldn't you have handled us alone?"

"I didn't bring Dennis. He was questioning me yesterday

about the work that's been going on up here. So I wanted to flag you off before he caught you at it. But it looks like he followed me tonight.''

He helped her up. She was an exceptionally pretty and shapely girl, right at the hour of a young woman's prime. Her skin was beautiful, her eyes a clear sea-blue, her features fine.

''Why should he follow you?'' she demanded. ''What's Tom Haines care what you do, long as you pay your rent?''

''Because I'm also supposed to pay a percentage of what I take out. It wouldn't look good if I were caught trying to hold out on him. But that's not what Dennis is after—he's hunting bigger game than that.''

''How big?'' asked the girl, skeptically.

''About the size of my partnership with Tom Haines,'' Freeman said grimly. ''Haines will close his Seven-Eleven mine when we open the new one, and Dennis will be out of a job. They say he made some wrong guesses in Seven-Eleven, so the chances are Haines won't be using him in the new one. Naturally he'd like to see his boss back out of the deal with me, so he can hang on at the other mine until he finds the vein he lost.''

''Maybe I'm not very quick, Mr. Freeman,'' the girl said. ''Why would Tom Haines back out just because Bill Croft's been taking nickels out of his sugar-bowl?''

''Because if he thinks I'm *letting* him steal nickels—as a bribe for giving my mine a good report—he's going to suspect there's something wrong with the mine! That's what Dennis will try to convince him of, at least.''

Smiling haughtily, the girl said: ''Oh, I don't think anybody would accuse you of favoring us. You haven't even taken down your *Keep Off* signs since Dad made his appraisal...''

Shepley's chin jutted. ''I didn't ask him to appraise it, much as I appreciate the good report. I'm selling a silver mine—not somebody's opinion of it.''

''But somebody's bad opinion would have killed the deal.''

Down the hill, Dennis was bawling: ''Are you coming

down, Freeman, or am I coming after you?"

"Keep your shirt on!" Shepley shouted. "—Yes, ma'am," he told Drusilla politely, "I'm obliged to Bill, and I aim to make it up to him. But right now I can't even tip my hat to him without making Haines suspicious. Come on—let's get moving."

He gripped her arm, and now Dru saw more in him than the high-falutingness she had discerned before. Not that she'd been anxious to make friends with him, she who'd promised herself to marry out of the mines or not to marry at all. But there was something mighty lofty about a man who would read a book on the Travertine train, when there was a girl sitting across the aisle from him. Yet suddenly that bookishness was overshadowed by a gray-eyed toughness. His aggressive manner made her shrink. His face looked flat and craggy, like some rocky bluff that people would call Geronimo's Head.

Following him, she stumbled. "What—what do you want me to do, then?"

"Tell him the truth: That you're working on your own. Otherwise I'll lose out and your father may go to jail."

"He'll go to jail anyway."

"If there's a fine, I'll pay it myself," Freeman said curtly. Then, as if he felt he should soften it: "You see, this mine means everything to me. I don't know about your people, but mine have been living underground for so many generations we're developing cheek-pouches and an appetite for roots. But not this Freeman! I've got my heart set on living in the sunlight, and it'll take ten Charlie Dennises swinging pick handles to spoil my plans."

Dru glanced at his back as he preceded her down the trail. His long arms swung deeply, as though he carried a six-foot drill in each hand, and for all his slenderness you would hardly call him thin. Yet she was apprehensive for what might happen if he tackled Dennis, that bull of the mines. Any ordinary man would simply break himself against the superintendent like a stick against a rock.

They reached the botton of the hill. Seated disconsolately

on an old ore-car, Bill Croft, a burly-shouldered little man with a head as bald as a tombstone, was glumly inspecting the broken shank of the wooden leg Charlie Dennis had shot off. Three feet away, tall, shirt-sleeved and grim, the superintendent held his gun on him. Near by, Croft's oil-barrel furnace snapped as it cooled.

Dru touched her father's shoulder. "Are you all right?"

"For a man who just lost a leg," sighed Croft, "I'm in fair shape." He grinned, and a row of gold teeth glinted. Croft had more gold in his mouth and less in his pocket, he claimed, than any man in Arizona.

Dennis glanced at Shepley with sardonic satisfaction. "Turn around. Let's see what kind of hardware your're packing."

Shepley shrugged and turned his back, but Drusilla bridled. "Aren't we being brave, Mr. Dennis! Shall I turn, too?"

Shepley shot her a warning look, as the superintendent drawled: "Might not be a bad idea." The girl's skirts swirled, and Dennis said: "Thanks. You can both turn around again. I just wanted to see if your backs were as guilty as your faces. I've had my eye on the three of you all summer. I knew something was going on, but I thought I'd wait and see what you were cooking up. And when Freeman came in last month with a stack of assay reports and a big grin, I said to myself, 'Charlie, my lad, somebody's after Mr. Haine's money!' "

He seemed grimly pleased, a deep-chested, muscular man timbered like a mine; and like a mine he had a solid, no-nonsense look. His brow was a bony prominence like a bar laid above his eyes, and his mouth confused jeering with humor. He was a plain man who by reputation swore allegiance only to his trade, his employers, and his opinions; a forced-march general; a slave-master who could outwork all his slaves. Within what scaffolding of sinew and prejudice, he looked impregnable.

"Leave Freeman out of it," said Bill Croft wearily. "It's my party, not his. What's a miner to do when he can't drill the rock any more, or even muck out a drift?''

Dennis's mouth hardened. ''Still blamin' me for your pegleg, eh? Still spreadin' your dirty lie that I let the operators bribe the mine-inspector for a clean bill of health?''

''I never blamed you, Dennis,'' Croft said doggedly.

''Like hell! Get up. We'll borrow a handcar at Hornitos and be in Travertine in time for breakfast in jail.''

Freeman spoke up. ''That's not necessary, Dennis. Take the gold he's got and tell him to go and sin no more.''

With his toe, Dennis pushed a crucible lying on the ground. ''I'll take it, all right, when it's cool enough to handle. But I'll take you right now. Get up, Croft.''

''Why take Mr. Freeman?'' Dru demanded. ''He just happened to be stalking us, like yourself.''

Dennis's large, scarred hands made the rifle look fragile. ''Now come the lies,'' he said grimly.

Shepley shrugged. ''All right, I suspected something was going on; but I didn't have time to lay any traps, and I probably wouldn't have bothered anyway. I was too busy hammering away at these dumps for two dollars a day.''

''But that's all behind you,'' Dennis said, his iron-scale eyes scornful under a brow like a cold chisel. ''Now you're a big silver-mine operator. Diamond Jim Freeman. Like hell!'' he barked. ''Croft's got more metal in his teeth than'll ever be hauled out of that hill you're trying to sell Tom Haines!''

''It's a good claim,'' Bill Croft defended staunchly. ''Every day for four days I walked over it. I went into the shafts and tunnels. The *mulata* rock is thick as corks behind a saloon. And the *mulata* don't sleep alone, Dennis, any mining man knows it. *You* know it. It sleeps with the chlorides, do it not?''

Dennis poked the rifle at the Cornishman. ''And you keep your hand in the pocket of the man who paid you to say that! But it's Haine's money in his pocket.'' He swung on Shepley. ''I call that compound thievery! You bribe Croft with Haines's own money, then Croft tells the lie to fleece the man!''

''If it's a lie,'' Shepley said, ''Haines's own geologist

started it. He only called in Croft to get a Cousin Jack's blessing on it. Like a lottery player reading his dream-book before he buys a ten-cent ticket.''

''Ten-cent?'' said Dennis. ''A twenty-thousand dollar ticket! Oh, it's a great little claim—but it took Croft four days to find something good to say about it. How come, Croft? Don't the spirit move the waters for you any faster than that?''

A tiny doubt assailed Shepley as Croft was silent; and he saw Dru frown while her father fumbled with the splintered stump on his peg-leg.

''All mines ain't the same,'' Croft declared slowly.

''*Now* you're talking,'' snapped Dennis. ''This one's *really* different. We'll skim off the silver like chicken-fat for the first few hundred feet—and then we're in country rock and trash. If it's any good, why wasn't it staked out during the boom? It's only a half-mile from a stope where they took out a half-million dollars.''

''It wasn't located,'' said Croft, ''because it's in the Triangle, the stretch of country the cattlemen and miners fought over. The cattlemen won and kept 'em out. And after the fuss, silver started sliding, so nobody prospected it close. This mine could be worth a lot,'' Croft declared. ''I make it to be at least three hundred thousand.''

''And I make it to be conspiracy to defraud!'' Dennis retorted. ''Get on our feet. We're going to town.'' His big hand dropped on Croft's shoulder and pulled him up. Croft took a hopping step, tripped, and fell with a clatter onto a square of sheet-metal. Shepley caught Dennis's arm. As Dennis turned, he saw how the muscles of his shoulders meshed heavily and smoothly with his neck, like the withers of a bull.

''Leave him alone,'' he said. ''He can't go on one leg.''

A keen anticipation lighted the superintendent's face. ''You can't kill a Cousin Jack,'' he scoffed. ''Bet he makes a mile before I have to carry him.'' He set the rifle down, and turned to clamp both hands on Croft's shoulders and haul him up again. Shepley's hand closed on Dennis's wrist.

"Leave him alone, I said!"

Dennis turned like a door slammed fast, smashing the back of his fist across Shepley's jaw, setting himself and then slamming home a right. Shepley sat down, a ringing numbness in his head. Dully he looked up at the superintendent, and saw the heavy boot ripping at his belly. It was too late to roll from it. He covered himself with his arms and waited. He heard a loud *whack*, and Dennis grunted. A thick-soled boot scuffed across Shepley's forearm and raked his ribs. Dennis swore, lost balance, and fell to his knees. Twisting to look behind him, he shouted:

"Ah, you shrew! Stand away or I'll break your scrawny neck!"

Again Shepley heard the *whack*, as Drusilla Croft smashed the mine-boss's rifle like a broom across his back. She darted away, again, raising the carbine, and Dennis lunged after her. Shepley followed him in a scrambling crawl, landing on Dennis's back in a dive. They skidded along the ground. Face down beneath him, Charlie Dennis was as solid as a horse, his big frame packed with muscle.

"The gun!" Shepley panted. Dru hesitated, and he snatched it from her as Dennis bucked him off. But he wheeled fast, slapped his weight onto it. Dennis's face was jammed against the ground. The man pawed desperately at him, groaning and cursing.

"You can break a man's neck this way," panted Shepley.

"Can't you? I've broken them with my bare hands," Dennis growled.

Shepley bore down harder as the big man threshed. Dennis's right hand clawed at Shepley's eyes, and Shepley turned his face.

"Make you a deal, Dennis!" he panted.

"Toe to toe is the only deal we'll make!"

Dennis wrenched violently under the gun-barrel, but Shepley levered it down harder still, and the mine-boss hunched in agony.

"How'd you like to boss the Sweet Betsy when we open it?" Shepley asked.

"If you open it, it won't be with Tom Haines!"

"What if I open it with somebody else, and make a killing? How'll you look when it gets around that you argued Haines out of buying it? The gossip will feed Charlie Dennis to the bears."

Dennis's struggling slackened, as though he were molding his forces like a bullet. "That's been done already," he said bitterly. "Haines's geologists lost the vein, but Dennis takes the blame."

"Well, here's one you won't take the blame for. Haines picked the Betsy himself."

Dennis remained still. "Is that any cash in my jeans? How do I know I'd boss it?"

Bill Croft hunched closer, catching onto the plan. "Suppose I wander in tomorrow and mention your name to Haines," he said. "He's more gambler, that one, than he is miner. Suppose I say this is the kind o' mine when Charlie Dennis is in his glory? And it's true. As a man you ain't worth powder to blast you to hell. But as a miner I drink your health—which you'll lose the day you turn your back on your men."

Presently Dennis grunted. "There's four men in line for the job already—good ones, too. Of course if he picks his man like he did last time—"

"There was a brawl, eh?" laughed Croft. "Ten of them went in the ring together, Freeman—ten hungry job-hunters. They fought for thirty-six minutes by Haines's watch. But it was Charlie Dennis who walked out and signed the payroll. I heard Haines made enough in bets on that fight to buy a team of bay horses for his sister."

"Blacks," said Dennis. For a while he was silent; then: "All right, I'll trade with you, Freeman. That's not sayin' my neck wouldn't outlast your rifle. But a job's a job. Put my name in the hat, and there'll be no mention of you and your swindling friends."

3

SHEPLEY AND DENNIS ROSE, Dennis massaging his neck with both hands. "That's a good trick. I'll remember it."

"I know some more," Shepley smiled. "If you know your nerves, you can handle any animal in the world, including mine-bosses. I knocked out a steer one time. But you have to stand in the right place to do it."

Dennis pointed a finger. "This here's the truth, mister—if you ever stand in my reach again, it'll be the right place for me but the wrong place for you. Nerves!" he grunted. "You talk like a sawbones."

Shepley grinned. "I learned just enough in medical school to be dangerous, I've been told. Now that we understand each other, I can tell you something else: I sign with Haines in the morning. We start blasting Monday. I hope you'll be working for us."

"Not 'us'—'him'," retorted Dennis. "Tom Haines never bought less than control of anything in his life. He came here three years ago with fifty dollars and a beautiful sister. Now he controls three mining companies. He's got a rabbit's-foot for luck, sister Jessie to charm the opposition, and Jake Lund for a lawyer. God help you, Freeman. He'll pick your bones like a stewing hen. You'll end up mucking ore in your own mine."

He found the crucible Croft had dropped and tapped out the metal in it. He tested it for heat and dropped it in his pocket. Then he bent to retrieve something from the ground.

"Here's a scrap of peg-leg for you, Croft," he said. "Slightly bullet-marked, but try it for size . . . Hollow leg, eh?" he remarked, examining it with a frown.

From the core of the dowel which had been Croft's leg he pulled a bit of wadding. Several pellets dropped onto his palm. He grunted and looked up. "What's this?"

Croft's face set in a pattern of shock. He turned his gaze to his daughter, stricken. Drusilla calmly extended her hand. "Just his medicine. But don't *you* take it," she added. "The doctor said it'd rupture the heart of a normal man."

"Ah, that shovel-leanin'," sighed Dennis. "It's worn out many a miner before his time, eh, Croft? Suppose you try it without pills for a while," he said. "You look healthy enough to me." He flung the pills into the brush, picked up his rifle, and started down the gully.

Shepley watched the girl as Dennis disappeared. She appeared about to call something sharp after him, but repressed it and bit her lip. He felt sorry for her, with all her pride and prettiness, both going to waste. Sorry for her father, too, so he said:

"I'll see that you get a job you can handle, Bill, if you like."

"Under Dennis?" challenged the girl. "Thanks just the same!"

"Excuse my daughter," chuckled Croft. "Her heart's better'n her manners. I believe she worries about becoming an old maid. Nineteen already, and won't have a mining man near her, so the choice is small. What you could do for us, if you like," he went on, "is to make arrangements with Haines for me to go on with the work here, but paying the percentage."

"Fine, I'll talk to him. Now, suppose you wait here while I get my horse for you to ride back. You'll never fit a peg to that shank without tools."

"And I'd never walk on the other leg if I did," Croft

confessed. "Dennis did my knee no good when he threw me down."

"It wasn't necessary, that about my becoming an old maid," Drusilla said haughtily, when Freeman had gone for the horse.

Bill Croft began packing his bellows and crucibles in a crate. "Why not? I figured he might as well know how you felt about mining men, so he wouldn't be pestering you."

"It's not that," Dru argued. "It's just—" She shook her head. How could she explain, without hurting him, that it wasn't miners, but the life of a miner's wife, that she hated? She was sad for all the dead miners and their widows and orphans, sad for the thousands of feet of rock that separated the living ones. And she was outraged to realize that Shepley Freeman had studied medicine for a while—but had given it up to go back to the mines. He said he didn't like mining— but here he was doing it just the same!

Suddenly she asked: "What was the idea of the hollow leg? Wasn't that the stuff you use to make your leaching brine?"

"It was," sighed her father. "May Dennis break his own leg for throwing those pills away, for they were the last I had!"

Dru regarded him curiously. "But I thought it took all Uncle Virgil gives you each week to make the brine?" She was surprised at this unexpected slyness in her father.

"It does. But I was holding back a few in case he should die on us..."

"Three pills? What use would they be?"

"A chemist could have analyzed them for me so I could make up my own. I should have done it before, but whoever I took them to might have got onto it, and spoiled the whole thing. And besides, Virgil is my own brother, whatever else the old rascal may be. "Well," he sighed, "you'll have to go in my place tomorrow. I can't travel on legs like these. How you'll explain to him that we don't have anything to show for the week's work, I don't know."

Each week Bill Croft visited his brother, turned in half the week's receipts, and got another supply of the mysterious pellets. Dusty federal warrants with Virgil Croft's name on them were floating about, so that he had to live across the border from Travertine in a Mexican village called Tintown. A miner by trade, a chemist by hobby, he had marketed a denture cement years ago which poisoned his customers. Judgments piled up, the law came after Uncle Virgil, and now he had to live in Mexico.

But there was nothing wrong with the gold-refining process he had discovered. Out of the exhausted concentrates of Hornitos it teased more gold than it seemed possible they contained. Once the process got out, he claimed, every old mine-dump and mill-tailing in the country would have miners swarming over it. Yet it took money to lease such properties, and that was what they were saving for—nibbling away by night at the old, rusty slides, and making just enough so that by the time they divided with Virgil Croft and paid a little on their bills in Travertine, there was nothing left. But Virgil Croft, part genius, part lunatic, suspiciously doled out just enough pellets for another week's work. That was how much he trusted his younger brother. Drusilla relished a visit with him like she would a spell of the measles.

4

FROM THE WINDOW of his lawyer's office, Tom Haines gazed down on Travertine. He liked this dusty mining town in the scorched hills of the border, where the sun fell sharply into the gulch between the adobe buildings, and miners' hovels of sheet-metal and adobe perched upon the slaglike slopes above the town. It was almost noon. The town murmured below the window—an empty wagon jarring along, the far, flat *clink* of a blacksmith's hammer, dogs yapping. High in a sky like blue glass, buzzards rode the rim of an invisible wheel. You liked any town where you had been lucky, he supposed, and he had been lucky here. In three years, he had driven himself into Travertime like a silver wedge. He had won some mining stock his first night in town; borrowed on it to buy a mine which oozed silver like mercury before it dried up—and even then he saw it coming, and had time to sell out before it happened. All you needed was guts and luck. Guts to buy while silver was falling; luck to keep your finger on those elusive veins of silver, and now and then to win at the gambling tables.

But sometimes you lost the luck as you lost the vein. A month ago Tom Haines had almost concluded that his luck had run out. Though he controlled three of the biggest mines in the area, silver had sagged below what it cost to mine it, and he'd had to close all but his Seven-Eleven mine, which Charlie Dennis managed to nurse along by making one miner do the work of two. And then Shepley Freeman had walked into his office.

As he would walk in presently this morning. It was a buyer's market, and Haines was buying control of the Sweet Betsy for a song—and a song was approximately what he had in the bank now. Freeman's Sweet Betsy would pay the bills until the Free-Silverites took Congress next fall. Then silver would hit the top, and Haines would reopen all the mines and buy up every marginal mine in Arizona. The name of Thomas Kevin Haines would be a star to set your compass by in Western mining. If Free-Silver didn't win—well, maybe he could ride it out on the Sweet Betsy alone....

Now, across the street and a hundred feet south, a corpulent man in a black suit left the bank with a black-haired girl of twenty. The girl popped open a parasol and the man held it for her as they came across the street. She said something and her laughter rang gay as a bell. She had the richest skin, the largest eyes, and the vividest lips in Arizona, Tom Haines thought. He was proud of his sister Jessie. She could soften a man faster with a smile than he could with a meat-ax; could get him bragging about his bankroll until they knew exactly where his power ended and his bluff began.

"Here they come!" said Jake Lund, Haines's lawyer. He was standing at another window, a tall man who looked like a Scandinavian lumberjack. Lundi's eyes were blue and his face meatless. "Brickwood wouldn't be coming, Tom, if he wasn't putting up the money."

"He had to put it up," Haines said. "He's got stock in everything I own. If I go under, his bank goes under. There'll be something besides wires hanging from the light-poles *that* day!"

Grinning at Lund, he flipped a nickle-sized goldpiece. Tall, well-made and Indian-haired, Tom Haines did credit to the black-and-gray suit he wore. His shoulders filled the coat, his legs were long and strong. Just shaven, his jaws had a bluish shine. Haines exhaled a worldly odor of bay rum and whisky. His gray eyes met the world frankly, whether he was counting the spots on a marked deck or reading the words in a hymnal in his and Jessie's pew Sunday morning.

He heard Carl Brickwood's boots and Jessie's high heels take the stairs. Lund seated himself at a desk which held a typewriting machine resembling a bird-cage, and began tapping importantly at it. On the checkered linoleum floor were arranged a roll-top desk, a case of ore samples and some leather chairs.

Jessie Haines entered with a smile for the lawyer and her brother. In her dove-gray gown with its prim white collar, she had a watch-charm delicacy—innocence with loaded dice in her purse, thought Haines. Brickwood followed her inside and scowled as he began fumbling for the trigger to collapse the parasol.

"I thought I'd say hello to Carl while I was in the bank," Jessie said brightly. "He was just coming up to see you, Tom. He said he'd have been put out if you hadn't let him buy some stock."

"Now wait!" Brickwood blurted. "I said I'd talk about it."

Glancing at the banker's florid face, Haines knew a fight was unavoidable. Changing his plans, he jabbed sharply at him. "Well, you took your time getting ready to talk," he declared. "Freeman's due in fifteen minutes."

Brickwood's yellowish eyes locked with his. In his lumpy black suit, he resembled a dressed-up bear. A high collar lacerated his jowls; lodge rings and buttons glittered on his lapels, vest and fingers. He must belong to everything except the Girl Reserves, thought Haines.

"As a matter of fact," Brickwood retorted, "I'd made up my mind not to go into the thing at all."

Jake Lund's chair creaked. Again Haines flipped and caught the coin.

"Up to you, Carl," he said. "I'll tell you where you're going if you don't go into the Sweet Betsy, though: to prison."

Brickwood's color deepened with a surge of red. "You've

got your brass-bound—!''

"Tom!" exclaimed Jessie. "How can you say such a thing to Carl?" She was seldom surprised, but now her neat, provocative features were startled.

"Drive down and meet Freeman at the station," Haines told his sister.

"No! I want to know why—"

Haines put a dry and somber stare on her, and though the rebellion remained in her face, she obediently turned to leave. As she passed the banker, she tapped his shoulder, smiling reprovingly. "Old bear," she murmured. "Hackles down. Tom's joking."

Haines heard her humming to herself as she descended the stairs. He went to a bookcase and drew out a cowhide-bound volume. "Let's see . . . Arizona Crimminal Code—ever get time to read, Carl? I've marked a reference on the mishandling of funds . . ."

"Mishandling! Because I put bank funds into your mines?"

"Read it."

Brickwood clamped his jaws and opened the book Haines handed him. At once his attention went to the bookmark—a canceled check. "What's this?" he demanded. "When did you ever give me five hundred dollars?" Flipping it over, he scowled at the notation on the reverse. " '*Received payment in full,*' " he read slowly, " '*for one hundred shares stock in Seven-Eleven Mining Company.*' Hell!" he exploded, "that was that stock you bought back from me two years ago!"

"Right. But you hadn't paid for it."

"Of course not! It was a bonus for—for investing some bank money in the mine!"

Jake Lund came in. "A bonus to an officer of a bank is illegal, Carl. I found that out later. You shouldn't have taken the stock—especially when you meant to convert it to cash right away."

"But Tom told me he wanted the stock back!" shouted Brickwood.

"Oh, now Carl," laughed Lund. "You knew it was a

reward—a bribe, I suppose the Criminal Code would call it.''

The banker's brow gathered into damp creases. He sat on the edge of a leather chair and held the volume on his lap. ''This is pretty rough, Tom,'' he accused numbly.

''It'd have been pretty rough to let me go broke, too.''

''But if I keep on plugging good money after bad into your companies—''

''Didn't you read the figures I gave you?''

Brickwood flapped a hand. ''Suppose the mine's as rich as you say—the bank's share of the half you're buying still wouldn't warrant the risk.''

''What about a share of *all* of the mine?''

''Freeman wouldn't sell it. If he did, we couldn't afford it.''

''He's selling a hundred percent, only he doesn't know it yet. We're *buying* fifty-one percent. We *take* the other forty-nine when he can't make his share of a payroll or a bill for supplies.''

''Uh...?'' Brickwood said.

Damn his thick head, thought Tom Haines. *Do I have to write it out?* ''We'll hit this mine fast, Carl,'' he explained, clenching his fist. ''Right off the bat we'll buy all the supplies we need for a year. We'll sink the shafts so fast it'll look like a prairie-dog town. Naturally the ore will pile up faster than we can mill it. So it'll be all outgo, no income at all. Freeman's got to match us, dollar for dollar. He'll go broke in a month.''

Brickwood gloomily wagged his head. ''Pretty rough, Tom. Pretty rough!''

''What's rougher than bankruptcy?'' Haines bridled. ''What's rougher than Yuma prison? Ask Johnny Keeley, at the Two Nations Saloon, about Yuma!''

''We could get burned,'' the banker predicted. ''Freeman's no dancing-master. He'll raise hell.''

''Johnny Keely's no dancing-master, either. We'll carry him as paymaster—in case.''

Staring into the dusty street, Brickwood muttered, ''I don't like it. Deals like that and men like Keeley will get us a bad reputation. You can hear dice rattle every time he moves.''

Johnny Keeley was a faro-dealer, arrogant and lazy, but good company, and the pearl-handled Colt he wore was more than an ornament. ''We'd get a worse reputation,'' Haines said, ''if Freeman got proddy and we had to handle him personally.''

The office grew quiet. Brickwood's lumpy shape blocked the window as he gazed into the street. At last he turned. Slowly, like a sleepwalker, he moved toward the door. Haines's heart stroked with alarm. It was true he could break the banker if he refused to take chips in his game; but by staying out, Brickwood would also break him.

''Well, are you in or out?'' Haines challenged.

Brickwood turned quickly, his red face bitter. ''Oh, I'm in! I'm in! I wouldn't miss it.''

He opened the door. Two steps below the landing, Tom Haines saw Jessie standing, a look of shock on her face. ''Would you hand me my parasol, Carl?'' she asked quickly. ''I had to come back for it.''

Brickwood handed it to the girl. ''Jessie!'' Haines called. But Brickwood closed the door with a bang.

Haines's long legs carried him swiftly to the door. Jessie was already halfway down the stairs on Brickwood's arm. ''Jessie,'' Haines repeated, ''I want to talk to you.''

Silhouetted against the dazzling gold of the street, the girl hesitated. ''Go on, Carl,'' she murmured. ''I guess I've go to talk to this brother of mine.''

''Jake, go get Johnny Keeley for me,'' Haines told Lund. As Lund departed, Haines led Jessie to a chair and seated her. She looked up with defiant eyes, her ruby ear-rings glowing against the warm olive of her cheeks. The crisp white collar of her dress gave her a schoolgirl look, but she had a woman's deviousness and her claws were sharp.

''Is this keyhole-listening a new talent?'' he asked.

''Brand new. Poor Carl! He didn't know the check was loaded.''

''He loaded it himself. You notice he was gambling with bank funds—not his own.''

"It was still a contemptible trick. You always told me you played a straight game—that the odds would take care of the honest gambler. How long have you been lying to me?"

"I'm not lying to you. I never have. But this isn't poker, Jess—this is how the mining game is played."

"You couldn't give Freeman a fair share of his own mine and do well enough?"

"We need every ton of ore in that mine to make out ourselves," Haines said earnestly.

"Then why don't we quit? We've got cash in the bank."

"Cash," sighed Haines, "is just a word tacked up behind the counter. We owe everybody in town. We're behind, Jess—way behind. But when silver goes up, we're king and queen of Arizona mining."

Jessie's lip pushed out. "What's a queen got besides a crown?"

"Money, for one thing. Something you're not going to have unless we get this mine." He looked at her appraisingly. "You're a beautiful woman, Jess. But girls just as beautiful are working in places you wouldn't pass without crossing the street. If I hadn't taken care of you after the folks died, you might be working in one of them yourself. You might land in one still, if we don't get this mine. It seems to me you owe me a little consideration, as well as yourself."

Jessie rose angrily and slapped him. Haines stepped back, startled.

"Is that what you were doing—taking care of me?" she snapped. "While I was finding out who had the money in the river towns so you wouldn't dull your shears on the wrong lambs? That was the tightest rope I'd ever want to walk, Tom. I almost got my throat slit a few times, by men I'd made fools of."

Haines's eyes were smoky. "It was rough for both of us. You might have got your throat slit—I might have got shot. I wouldn't want to go back to it. Would you?"

Doubt drifted across her face. "Why should we have to? We can always sell the stock we hold in the other mines."

"Sell stock in closed-down mines? That's what I've been

talking about. We owe money all over town! Unless silver goes up again, we're broke. So we've got to have that mine."

Jessie turned away. "This is worse than anything we ever did before. At least they had a chance, Shepley hasn't."

A thought struck Haines. His eyes narrowing, he asked: "There's nothing personal in this feeling of yours, is there? You did spend a little time setting him up—going to lunch with him when I was busy, and so on. Believe me," he laughed, "he's just a lucky mining bum, Jess! Probably never got past fourth grade."

"Oh?" Jessie's brows went up. "He was going to medical school when he ran out of money."

"Medical school! *Freeman?* He's got hands like hams and probably a brain like a buffalo!"

Her chin up, Jessie insisted, "His father made him finish school, while Shep worked summers. Everybody in the family scrimped so they could have a white-collar man to boast about. Then his father died and he sank what was left in those old tailings. He told me he'd be ten years paying people back if he ever makes it."

Haines broke out laughing. He took his sister by the shoulders. "Who's using the shaved deck on who? I'd better have another look at this gopher hole before I buy it. I'll ask Doc Wilson about him. Bet he never got closer to medical school than a bottle of serpent-oil liniment!"

Jessie tore away. She snatched her handbag from the desk and marched to the door. It slammed behind her.

Now Haines relaxed, for he knew her: If you could crack open a little wedge of doubt, she'd take it the rest of the way, fearing she'd been made a fool of. Freeman might have quite a time ahead of him, yet...

A moment later he hear a man sauntering with a jingle of spurs up the stairway. The door opened and Johnny Keeley touched the brim of his Stetson as he entered. "Salutes," he said. "Lund says we're in business."

"Mighty close to it. Is Charlie Dennis around?"

"He was eating breakfast an hour ago. Up late with a sick mine, he said."

Keeley, wearing no coat, hooked his thumbs in the pockets of his yellow vest and spaced his boots wide. Haines catalogued the things which were wrong with him: Hair and sideburns too long; skin sallow and cheeks sunken; black pants too tight. Dice bulged in the pocket of his vest and his pearl-handled Colt was too obvious. But his ability to use the gun, and his self-assurance, were impeccable.

"Find him and tell him this," Haines said crisply: "I've got three other men looking for Charlie's job. So I'll settle it like last time: in the street."

Keeley's brow lifted. "Charlie was tellin' me about that. Thought he was just blowin'." His eyes were puzzled, faintly critical, and Haines said shortly:

"First and last, a mine-boss is a bruiser—the toughest bruiser in the mine. If he's afraid of a little action, then by God he better get into another trade."

"Mother always said that," Keeley said solemnly. Then, grinning: "We could make a killing on this fight. Get Charlie to lose—and let me put a roll on somebody else to win."

"Charlie'd rather die than lose a fight. Time's short, Johnny, but here's what I want you to do. Get Freeman into the ring with Dennis after he polishes off the others. There's only three of them, and Charlie will probably pick up one to use as a club on the others."

"Freeman! He ain't hard-up enough to work in his own mine, is he?"

"No, but he may need some softening up before we start mining. Charlie would be a good man to wield the cleaver. How you get Freeman into the ring is up to you. As his partner I'd better stay on the sidelines."

Keeley frowned at a fleck of mud on his boot, and rubbed it off on his trouser leg. "Where do I see him?"

"At the Two Nations Saloon, right away. I'm going down and wait for him. Find Charlie and bring him too. We'll sign the papers and see what develops after that."

5

As THE NARROW-GAUGE TRAIN lurched and rattled toward Travertine, Shepley Freeman tried to read Strumpel's *Practice*. Three times a week the train smoked down from Tucson to Travertine, on the border, making a flag-stop at Hornitos. For the occasion, the biggest of his life so far, he had put on his town clothes—a brown suit with small lapels, a starched collar, and tan shoes a trifle too tight for him—the outfit his mother had insisted on his having when he went East to medical school three years before. He felt somewhat foolish in it, but he wanted to be able to write her that he had worn it to the signing.

Occasionally, he raised the book to blow dust from the page. The rails ran through a jumble of dry foothills scarred with the claw-marks of erosion. Heavy yellow weeds grew close to the tracks; and on the hills, gray oak and huge moss-green mesquite trees made black puddles of shadow. Shepley closed the book. It was difficult to concentrate, with big things in the air and Drusilla Croft sitting a few seats ahead. He laid the book on the seat and groped down the galloping aisle to where she sat.

She looked up, not too hastily. She looked strikingly pretty today, with her nice blue eyes and golden hair. She always did her hair up for her trips to town.

"How is Bill?" he asked.

"Pretty lame, Mr. Freeman, thank you for asking."

"My friends call me Shep. So you're doing the shopping this week," he smiled. "And then you'll go over to Tintown to see your Uncle Virgil. Right?"

Her eyes widened a bit. "Yes. That's right."

He sat down. "What's the matter with Uncle Virgil? He never visits here—Bill always visits there. Doesn't he like Americans?" Getting comfortable, he slid his long legs under the seat ahead.

"Uncle Virgil finds it too clean over here," said Dru.

Smoke and cinders swept through the open windows as the train took a turn. The passengers leaned like horsemen. Dru put two fingers to her eye. "Fiddlesticks! I thought just *once* I might make it without a cinder in my eye! Now my nose will run and my eye will be red..."

"Lean back." Shep eased her head against the bristly plush and twisted a corner of his handkerchief. "So your eye gets red when you rub it. What do you expect, grinding the cinder into the tissues?"

Her lips eased into a smile. Satiny-rose, they looked delicious. "I believe you really did dabble in medicine," she murmured.

"Up to fourteen hours a day I dabbled."

"It got too hard for you, then?"

"No, I ran out of money after my father died. Even a shirttail school like I was going to costs money. And I had room and board to make, too." Removing the bit of carbon, he exhibited it thoughtfully. "Reminds me of you, in some ways, Miss Drusilla. Lots of sharp corners to irritate a person—"

Color deepened in her cheeks. She had the thin skin which blushes easily. "I'm a shrew, like Charlie Dennis said. But I'm thinking of the waste, Shep—throwing the chance to be a doctor down the dirty shaft of a mine!"

"I didn't throw it away. I told you I had to go to work. I've worked summers in the mines since I was fourteen. But the family picked me to stay in school because they had the idea of making a doctor out of me.''

"Oh, then it's a sort of hand-me-down ambition?'' She sounded disappointed.

"No, I came by it honestly. I used to bother the company doctor when I was a kid—clean his office and make splints for him out of yucca. Then I started borrowing books. I always knew I'd wind up in the mines, but I treated myself to dreams about saving the life of the mine-owner's son in a cave-in, and getting a scholarship for it.''

He chuckled at the memory, but an excitement had kindled in Dru's eyes. ''And now you've got your scholarship! Why, the money from Tom Haines will take you through school and get you started.''

Shep moved his feet, uncomfortably. ''Well, I'd be foolish to walk out before the mine's producing. If I don't stick around a while, it's liable to be somebody else's fortune the mine makes. After everything's started, I can go back to school.''

Dru's hands clenched in her lap. ''You must go back now, or you'll never go back.''

"Why not?''

"Do I need to tell you that—a miner's son? Because in the first place it will be somebody else's fortune anyway—the supply houses' and the miners. I—I must sound like the fox that couldn't reach the grapes. But it isn't that. I've seen so many mines start rich and end poor. And all the money the poor prospector got went into labor and machinery. And then what does he do? For the rest of his life he tramps around with a burro and a head full of foolishness.''

He rubbed his neck. She almost had him worried—with a fortune waiting for him! ''The geologists say the ledge will go down fifteen hundred feet.''

"And who'll make the fortune—you or Tom Haines? Dennis says he'll pick your bones.''

Shep inspected his hands, and closed them into fists. ''I come from large-boned people. They'll take some picking.''

Ahead he glimpsed the russet hills which sheltered Travertine. The gaunt outlines of old gallows-frames and ore-chutes

loomed among the closed-down mines. They rattled past a
stockyard and slaughter house, where buzzards sat naked-
headed on the sheet-metal roofs. With a bleat of the whistle,
the train pulled into a station with a yellow depot under a
turquoise sky, a strip of dreary grass, and a dripping water-
tower. He rose, and to his surprise Dru caught his hand and
smiled; and her lips were as beautiful smiling as in that grave
repose.

"The blessings of the tommyknockers on you, then—and
that's the finest thing a Cousin Jennie can wish a man. We're
savin' folk, and we hate to see a good man wasted."

A HOT WIND was raking up the tracks from Tintown, the
Mexican village across the line. Before the depot a girl in a
gray gown was holding her skirts down as the breeze whipped
at them. She came toward them as they dismounted.

"I'm to deliver you into Jake Lund's hands," Jessie
Haines told Shepley importantly. "Drusilla, can't we drop
you somewhere?"

"No, thanks. I have to see about a package." She walked
abruptly into the baggage room.

Before the station, at the foot of the street which climbed
steeply to the business district, a buggy waited with a beauti-
fully groomed black in the shafts. "You drive," Jessie said.
Shep handed her into the buggy, laid his dusty medical book
on the floor, and took in the anchor. "Tom's waiting in Jake
Lund's office," she said. "Just loaded with good things for
you."

After I get to know her better, he thought, *I'll know when
she's joking and when she isn't*. Just now he didn't. He
asked, "Good things like money?"

"Very similar, at least." She smiled quickly at him and
then looked back at the road. There was a fetching, rather
exotic slant to Jessie's eyes. Her nose was a bit short, her
lower lip full, and there was an olive richness to her skin, a
warm sheen. About her there was something wistful, as if,
brought up in an adult world of success and cigar smoke, she
had missed some fun she still hoped to enjoy.

In no hurry, savoring the moment despite his tight shoes and snug coat, Shep let the horse walk. Travertine, with its rusty roofs, large but flaking store-signs, and mis-aligned electric-light poles, had a disconsolate look. It had grown wealthy when silver was competing strongly with gold to be the legal monetary standard; but now the flourishes to which it had treated itself were more than it could maintain. In a few years, if silver kept sliding, it would go bankrupt, like Hornitos. His own good fortune kept him from feeling sincerely sad about it.

"Did you try anywhere for financing before you came to Tom?" Jessie asked him.

"Sure. Everywhere. But the offers sounded like insults."

"I'm glad you did, Shep, because mining isn't the place for a man in a hurry. What will you do with all that money?"

"Well, I'll squander the first few hundred on girls, of course. The rest I'll nail down where I can find it when I need it."

"Why don't you nail it down at that medical school you were telling me about?"

Shep laughed wryly. "Everybody wants me to get out of town! What's the matter with me?"

Jessie smiled. "I'm thinking of all the mines that opened like grand opera, and expired like Little Eva. Maybe you should just give Tom a bill of sale on the whole thing and let him worry about whether he makes any money."

Shep frowned at her neat profile. "That mine's worth a quarter of a million, Jessie. Would *you* sell it for twenty thousand?" He wondered suddenly if this was a last-minute strategy initiated by her brother.

"No mine is worth any more than they take out of it," Jessie said.

The shaft-horse shied as a man stepped from the high boardwalk. He had been sitting in the deep alcove of a window, and Shep had seen him discard a cigarette and lounge forward as the buggy approached. He carried himself as if he was either very tired or very lazy, his hands tucked into the hip pockets of his tight black trousers. He wore a lemon-yellow vest of soft leather, and a gray Stetson was cocked over one eye. "Keep driving!" Jessie said under her breath. But the man reached up to catch the harness as Shep shook the lines.

"Hey—where you goin' with that pretty girl?" He grinned. "That's *my* girl—ain't that so, Rabbit?"

"Every girl's your girl, Johnny Keeley," said Jessie. "You old tom-cat."

"Why, just listen to her!" laughed the faro-dealer. Noting the knoblike cheekbones, pasty skin and gaunt jaws, Shep made a quick diagnosis: T.B., probably contracted in prison, and made worse by cigarettes, whisky, and the rank air of gambling rooms.

"Excuse us, Johnny," he said. "Somebody's waiting."

Keeley gazed raptly at Jessie, ignoring Shep. "Man, ain't that stuff pretty?" he breathed.

Jessie's chin went up. When Shep stirred forward, she touched his knee quickly as if in warning. "I suppose you're out making book for the fight, you lazy thing," she told Keeley.

"What fight's that, now?" Keeley asked innocently.

"The one Charlie Dennis is going to win tonight."

"Oh, *that* fight." Releasing the horse, Keeley pressed a bullet up out of his gunbelt and scratched his sideburn with the nose of it. "Naw, nobody's bettin'! Who'd bet against a pat hand like Charlie? Here I am with two hundred dollars in my jeans, and nobody will bet with me. Man, if I could just find a dark horse to run against him—"

"What about yourself?" asked Shep. "Maybe you could handle Charlie."

"Well, I'm a little out of condition just now. What about you?"

"Don't look at Shep," said Jessie. "He's in the business end of it."

"Me too," said Johnny Keeley. "Your brother's hired me for paymaster. Charlie was tellin' us you've got a theory about knockin' out large animals like cows, Freeman—something about mashin' a nerve, wasn't it?"

"Sounds like Charlie's been talking out of turn," Shep retorted. He gave the lines a shake, but again Keeley held the horse.

"Mister Tom Haines is waitin' on you in the saloon," he explained finally. "Him and Jake Lund and Charlie. They got all the papers and stuff. Just waitin' on you. Come on in."

"That brother of mine!" exclaimed Jessie. "Go on, Shep; I'll take the buggy."

Shep frowned at the rusty beer-shields beside the saloon door, and the colored paper, representing stained glass, which was peeling from the lower windowpanes. A little of the pleasure of the morning went out of him. Signing papers in a saloon was less grand than the scene he had pictured. He dismounted, feeling foolish in his town clothes.

"Good luck," Jessie smiled. "Oh—something I forgot to ask. Where did you go to medical school?"

Shepley looked at her. "A little place in Nashville. Whitford College. Who's asking?"

"A curious female. Oh—" She leaned down to retrieve the book he had laid on the floor. "Don't forget this." As she handed it to him, she glanced at the title. "'Strumpel's *Practice*.' Good!" she said, and drove up the street.

"Let's go, Professor," said Johnny Keeley.

6

THE TWO NATIONS SALOON WAS RUN by a man named
Fletcher Henry, nicknamed Fletch. The saloon was dark and
musty, full of curiosities like stuffed eagles, rattlesnakes and
Gila monsters, and even an Indian mummy. Though times
were bad, this noon found a crowd of miners gathered about
the four men at a round, green-topped table in front, as they
signed the papers to bring the Sweet Betsy mine into being.

Haines's signature on the documents took up so much
space that there was little room for Shep to sign below. He
pushed his name through the copperplate flourishes and
handed the pen to Jake Lund to witness. Lund scratched at the
papers and offered the pen to Charlie Dennis. Then the papers
came back to Tom Haines, black-haired, dominant, smiling,
who separated the copies, affixed a bank-draft to one and
handed it to Shep, rising as he did so.

"How's Monday for the ground-breaking?" he asked,
offering his hand. In Shep's grip his fingers were uncallused,
but with strength and hardness beneath the skin.

"Seven o'clock." He glanced at the check. "I expect this
will buy a drink for everybody, won't it?"

"My party," Haines insisted, moving toward the bar.
"Every man that can hold a glass—belly up to the bar! A
mine is about to open—for a change!"

As they drank, Shep lost count of the men who paused by Charlie Dennis to murmur: "Don't forget me Monday, Mr. Dennis!" To each of the miners, the superintendent would mutter:

"Talk to the boss-man! I'm just drinking here. I'm out of work myself."

Finally Shep said to Haines: "Who's going to ramrod this mine?"

Haines stacked some coins on the bar. "That's up to Charlie. Depends on whether he's man enough to take the job away from the other men who want it. How about it, Charlie?" He shot a look at the superintendent.

Standing at Shep's left, Dennis pushed his hat back. The scarred brown features eased into a grin of pleasure. "I'm your boy! I'd sooner fight that write a letter of application any day."

"Atta boy," said Haines, reaching past Shep to slap him on the back. "These other three fellows will probably back out anyway. But I'll bet we separate the men from the boys. How do you figure his chances, Johnny?"

Keeley came around to feel Dennis's biceps and shake his head. "Don' know . . . kinda seems to me like Charlie's past his prime. How old are you, Charlie?"

Dennis swore and hauled back his shirt sleeve, baring a great, corded, milk-white biceps. "Forty-four—same caliber as your Colt!" he said.

Haines laughed. "My money's on Charlie," he said.

But now Keeley was solemnly laying on the bar a heavy clothbound volume. With a gripe of irritation Shepley saw that it was his *Practice*. Keeley opened it, licked his fingers and turned a few pages.

"Mine ain't," he said. "I've got this-here dark horse, see? He's more of a think-fighter than a fist-fighter, but he says he's real good. Where's the chapter on licking large animals like Dennis?" he asked Shep suddenly.

The laughter came like an explosion. But as Shep pulled the book from Keeley's hands the crowd grew silent, impatient to hear what he had to say. And he remembered how greedily people took you up on anything you said which might be construed as a boast.

"I said some animals could be put out of action if you knew the nerves," he retorted. "A deer-hunter picks his spot; so does a bullfighter. Nothing new in that."

"But the trouble with using that system on Dennis," said Tom Haines, "is that he hasn't got any nerves. Where would you hit an animal like him?"

Shep looked at him, then at Dennis, who looked as if he had just found a marvelous gift beneath the Christmas tree. "When is this brawl?"

"Tonight," said Haines. The room was still.

"Would it make sense for me to tangle with Charlie and three other men for a job I don't want?"

"You remind me of an Injun I used to know," Dennis prodded. "The tribe called him Big Talker."

Again there was laughter. The bartenders kept dipping glasses and pouring liquor, the miners kept drinking, but they were all restless to see the fight set up. Shep recalled the mulish strength of Dennis during that savage moment at the mill. He studied the big man with a thoughtful gaze; but suddenly he removed Dennis's hat and laid it on the bar. There was a stir. Dennis flinched as Shep put his hands on the sides of his shaggy, bull-like head and gazed straight into his eyes. Shep let his hands slide down over the ears to the neck, felt the cords of it, dug his thumbs into Dennis's shoulder-sinews, and finally let his hands fall away.

"I don't know," he said. "I think he might react pretty well to a blow to the carotid sinus. He looks like the carotid type."

Dennis flushed and was going to say something, but Tom Haines chuckled: "Not Charlie. Charlie's the bull-buffalo type. Meaning no disrespect to you as a professional man, Shep—but in case you get nerved up to fight him, I'm giving Johnny Keeley five hundred dollars to bet for me. On Charlie."

"It'll go beggin'," bragged Dennis.

Shep had the feeling that his new partner had engineered

the whole party—had put speeches in Keeley's and Dennis's mouths—and that it was all for his own entertainment and that of his friends when Dennis fought under the gaslights in the street tonight. He knew how much respect he would command in his own mine when it was advertised that he was afraid of his superintendent.

"All right," he announced. "I'll take him on. And I'll back up my professional opinion with five hundred dollars."

"How's that?" Haines asked, to be sure what he meant.

"I mean I won't fight him for nothing, but I'll give Fletch Henry my check for five hundred dollars to bet on me at ringside odds."

He shoved away from the bar, but Charlie Dennis came after him. "Hey, Doc! Don't forget your book. I figure you've got a lot of readin' to do between now and seven o'clock."

After Shepley Freeman left, Fletch's place became noisier and more jovial than it had been in many months. Drinking sturdily, Charlie Dennis promised a job to every miner who could reach his side. He was feeling flushed and hectic when he got a signal from Tom Haines. Dennis left the bar and Haines took him over near the mechanical pianos, where the clatter was fiendish. Haines looked steady and cool, and Dennis wished he had not drunk so much.

"Assuming you get the job, Charlie—how many men do you plan to take up there Monday?"

"These days one man'll work like two," Dennis said. "Twenty-five or thirty will get us started."

"Better make it a hundred and fifty," Haines said.

"A hundred and fifty! It's wastin' your money, Mr. Haines. They'll be falling all over theirselves."

"There'll be enough work for everybody. Leave that to me. I'm starting this one big to take advantage of slump prices and that ambition in miners you're talking about. After November, when Free Silver takes control of Congress, things will skyrocket. Take a hundred and fifty men up there, and let's see the dust fly. In the meantime," he said, "you'd better go to your place and rest up. And no more liquor until after the fight."

Feeling foolish and humiliated, Charlie Dennis departed. He was sober enough to resent the way he was being hired; drunk enough to bridle at being told he was drinking too much. The sudden glare of the street made him shade his eyes. The liquor in him partly buoyed him up, partly stupefied him, and he shambled up the street, turned a corner and struggled along a stony road without sidewalks toward his boarding-house halfway up a flinty hill. He leaned against an adobe wall to whip a match across his hip, muttered when it broke, and struck another. He drew at the flame with the dark tube of a cigar, thinking bitterly and contemptuously of Shepley Freeman.

Last month he'd been just a tramp miner trying to scrounge gold from the cement-heaps of Hornitos. Today he had his foot in that world of clean faces, short hours, and girls like Jessie Haines who gave you their hands to fondle and said, smiling, "Won't you come to dinner soon? And do bring your checkbook—we'll read it together."

Into his throat rose a corroding envy. He had forgotten more about mining than Freeman would ever know. But Freeman had blundered into the Sweet Betsy ledge like a drunk falling into a mine-shaft, and had come out covered with silver.

Whereas Charlie Dennis was caught like a fly in that thin layer of mining society between the frosting at the top and the soggy stuff at the bottom. Too good for the kind of woman and liquor of which the miners partook, not good enough to appreciate the sour bilge called Scotch which Tom Haines drank, nor to get his hands on a girl like Jessie. His attempt to be friendly with her once had brought a stern bit of advice from Haines—she was the little golden bird he might crush.

So he held a rank like that of a warrant officer, entitled to a salute from the enlisted men, to condescending fraternization from the officers—provided he wasn't drunk. But in one jump, Freeman had made it from the bottom to the top— Freeman, with his books and great plans—painful reminders of Dennis's own days of studying half the night in an effort to improve himself. Life would have straightened Freeman out on *that* foolishness, had he not had the luck to sink his pick into a ledge of pure silver. A wave of jealousy smothered him. *By God, mister, I'll have my inning tonight, though!* He was shaken by the strength of his hatred. *By heaven,* he thought, *he'll be too sick a man for a week to enjoy that check! He'll lose his five hundred, and spend another hundred getting his front teeth repaired.*

The afternoon passed hurriedly for Drusilla Croft. But after dinner, she faced the inevitable: She must visit Uncle Virgil and Tintown, and get the week's supply of leaching-materials. After leaving her parcels at the railroad station, she crossed into the Mexican village, a withered little town with a suggestion of streets converging near the railroad. Some mescal shops and nameless stores were set among vacant lots where milch-goats grazed on wisps of grass, and pigs and chickens strayed untended. Virgil Croft lived in a shack a mile south. The day was still hot, and the girl was fanning herself with her bonnet before she sighted the adobe shack across the sandy bed of the Rio Arriba.

Reaching the far side, she could hear Uncle Virgil crooning to his chickens as he fed them. They were fighting cocks which he raised for sale in Sonora—vicious bronze-and-green birds with legs as thick as cornstalks. His relations with animals were much happier than his relations with people, it seemed to her.

"Uncle Virgil?" she called, stopping at the well. A stooped shirtless old man in overalls and Mexican sandals tuned quickly at her call. He had been throwing corn into the cages where the cocks were kept. A bantam rooster rode the rim of the pail he carried.

"You're late, niece," he announced. Carrying the pail, he led her to the shack. She was always uneasy with him. He was tight-lipped and forbidding. The withered leather of his upper arms slid around hard, rodlike muscles; but superimposed on this body of a hermit was the head of a scholar, high-domed, with wisps of white hair.

"It was hot in town," she said, explaining her tardiness. "I waited for it to cool."

"It's hotter in here."

Dru braced herself, took a last breath of fresh air, and entered the shack. Heat and liniment-smell assailed her. The adobe walls were dark with smoke. An old Springfield stood in a corner. Her gaze skimmed the narrow cot and rumpled blankets, the black overcoat hanging from a nail, the littered kitchen-corner.

"Ain't eaten, have you?"

"Oh, yes!"

"Well, have some custard. Just made it."

He set out custard speckled with ash from the oven, and a dirty spoon. Furtively she wiped the spoon on her skirt. "Not clean enough for you?" he grinned.

"There was a speck on it."

"There's a speck on everything worthwhile. 'The perfect,'" quoted Croft, "'is the enemy of the good.' How's brother? Ailing, I judge?"

"He wrenched his knee, so I came. You see, we're out of the pellets. And the awful thing is—"

"Have you got my money?"

"That's what I was going to tell you," Dru faltered. "Charlie Dennis caught us! He promised to keep it secret, but he took the gold we had. But Mr. Freeman, the man who holds the lease, is making arrangements so we can go on."

Croft's chair crashed as he sprang up. "God in heaven—! Now it'll be all over Travertine—all over the country—and they'll be soaking up all the leases and old mines. And I won't get a nickel out of them!"

"But Dennis doesn't know the process—!"

"He doesn't, eh? You didn't have the stuff analyzed and sell him the formula? It ain't that, now, is it?"

"Uncle Virgil!"

"Doesn't your thick-headed father know that as soon as it gets out that there's a new process, they'll be spying on us to find out what it is?" Kicking trash out of his way, he strode to an unglazed window and peered out, as if already he were under surveillance. "I should have sold it for cash in the beginning," he muttered.

"Perhaps you should still."

He turned back. "And lose a fortune? The real money goes to the man who holds the leases. But leases cost money, and I can't work the old ones down here, because they're in the Indian country, and the Yaquis are all over them like ants. And now my idiotic brother—"

"Don't call him an idiot!"

Croft frowned, surprised at her sharpness. "Hear me, Drusilla: I've spent ten years in filthy Mexican towns like this because of those judgments against me. For ten thousand dollars I could pay them off and go home. But if I didn't get any more than that out of it, I'd go home broke. And if I tried to sell it to somebody like that fellow Haines, he'd steal it from me. That's why I've had to cripple along with your father's miserable moonshining."

She was silent. The bantam flapped its wings. Croft chewed his lip. "You say Dennis didn't know what was going on?"

"He couldn't have. We were just using the furnace."

"And Freeman's fixing it so you can work again?"

"Yes. Maybe we can even sublet from him and work on a bigger scale."

Croft muttered something to himself and went to a corner occupied by a small, greasy range. From a row of cans on a spiceshelf, he selected a tobacco can and carried it to the table.

There. One week's supply. Never mind wondering where I keep the rest. But as God is my witness, if you fail me again I'll sell it for what I can get. Gettin' dark," he said. "You'd better get started."

He opened the door. Gazing over the scorched desert, he grumbled: "You'd think you'd get used to this country eventually, wouldn't you? You don't. You hate it more all the time. It's a scorpion-crawlin' prison. Go on before I change my mind and sell to that scoundrelly Tom Haines. And bring me the gold next time, not money—I'll divide it myself."

7

AT SIX-FORTY-FIVE, Shep Freeman sat in a room in the Montezuma Hotel. Both his hands were soaking in a basin of alum water to toughen them. He rose from the cot and shook them dry as he walked to the window. The street was nearly dark. Before the Two Nations Saloon the crowd stirred a dry haze that floated to the rooftops. A water-wagon came along laying the dust, and after it passed, some of Fletcher Henry's men got busy fashioning a rope-ring in the middle of the road.

Shep went to the washstand and washed his face. As he dried, he inspected himself critically in the mirror. He was too stringy to match Dennis for brute power. In any close fighting, the superintendent would maul him like a bear. Yet Shep was in better condition, and if he stayed away and shot at the nerve centers, coaxed Dennis into leaving himself open—he rolled a punch from the shoulder, threw the clincher to the solar plexus—that bulwark of muscle and beef would drop like a safe.

Downstairs he drank two cups of black coffee. He glanced at the clock: seven straight up. As he left the hotel he heard a roar from the crowd down the hill. Vaulting to a tie-rail, he saw that Charlie Dennis had come into the ring. Stripped to the waist, he had the dead-white look of unfired china under the hissing glare of a battery of mine-lamps. Three other men

were already there. Shirtless, uneasy, they watched while
Dennis strode about flexing his arms. Just below the ring a
haywagon was drawn up. Here Tom Haines, Johnny Keeley
and a dozen other men sat. Shep pushed on down the walk
and through the crowd to the wagon. As he climbed onto it, a
red-faced man in a silk hat came toward him.

"Wait a minute—wait a minute! This is for Mr. Haines's
friends—"

"That's my partner, Ira," Haines called with a smile. He
raised his hand toward Shep.

Shep answered with a hand-salute. Turning to gaze at the
crowd, he could see them judging him like a horse. He felt
nervous under that mass stare. A man flapped some
goldbacks in the air. "Five to one on Dennis!" In one corner
of the ring, Fletcher Henry, a tough little man in a derby and
striped jersey, was arranging buckets and bottles. The other
three men who were going to fight were standing near the
rope barrier across the ring. There was a tall handlebar-
mustached man in his late thirties who stood with his arms
crossed and one foot out, grimly confident. The others were
shorter and appeared out of condition. Nothing but hard times
could have prodded them into this ring, Shep thought.

Johnny Keeley carried a couple of bottles over to Shep.
"Better have a shot, boy. You look sick."

"Not as sick as I'd look with whisky in me."

Keeley laughed. Raising a bottle toward Dennis, he called,
"Hey, Charlie! Doc says this stuff is bad for you! Ever hear
that?"

Chewing on a cigar someone had handed him, the superintendent sauntered over, rolling his huge white shoulders. He
put up his hand for the bottle and tipped it up. "Whisky bad
for you?" he said. "Only if you get hit with the bottle." He
went back to touring up and down the rope, flexing his arms.

"Make it a good 'un," Keeley told Shep, in quick serious-
ness. "You're packin' a hundred bucks of Jessie's and two
hundred of mine."

Shep looked him over. "Shall I laugh now?"

Keeley mourned, "How can you pass up odds like five-to-one, even if you know you'll lose? I pick up a thousand if you're the last man on his feet.''

Fletch Henry was ringing a cowbell for quiet. Standing on the wagon, he bawled: ''The purse for this fight will be a fine job under Travertine's own Tom Haines. A man who cannot come up to the scratch within sixty seconds after a knockdown will be eliminated. The match will be between Travertine's own Charlie Dennis; John Allan, the Pride of Globe; Oscar Morris from Tombstone; Frank Magill from Nogales; and the battling physician from Hornitos—Shep Freeman! Boys, are you ready?''

Shep jumped into the ring. He walked to a corner as the three men across the ring separated. Dennis was in the corner opposite Shep. It was suddenly so quiet Shep could hear the fizzing of the carbide lights. Charlie Dennis scooped up some earth and stared across the ring at Shep. The cowbell's flat jangling startled Shep. He saw Dennis rushing toward him. The crowd yelled.

Then there was a scurrying of fighters from the other corners, and Dennis halted, pivoted, and cocked his fist as John Allan, the tall, mustached engineer from Globe, lunged at him. The other two fighters piled into Dennis from the right. A fist smacked into Dennis's back; there was a thud as Allan landed one to his face. Dennis roared and began smashing out at all three. It was clearly a pre-arranged battle-plan, and Dennis was bleeding from the nose as he gave ground. One of the shorter men worked around behind him and seized his arm.

''All right, hold him!'' Allan panted. While the third man tried to get behind Dennis from the other side, Allan measured and landed a clean shot to the superintendent's jaw.

I suppose I'm next, Shep thought, watching the terriers drag down the bull of the mines. He crossed the ring, caught Allan by the shoulder, and pulled him around. His fist hit in the middle of the surprised face. Allan went reeling into the ropes.

Dennis whirled on the man who was holding his arm. His fist cocked and rammed. The other man who had been harry-

ing Dennis came rushing at Shep from the side. Across the
ground Fletch Henry was bawling, "Timekeeper!" A man
ducked into the ring and began counting over the candidate
Dennis had just knocked down.

Shep landed a quick one to the red face of the man who had
been helping to harry the superintendent. Then John Allan
scrambled off the ropes and rushed Shep from the side. Shep
took the punch he threw, and pumped a bruising fist up under
Allan's ribs. Allan gasped, made a retching mouth, and sank
to his knees.

"*Timekeeper!*" A second timekeeper jumped into the
ring.

The red-faced man was flailing desperately at Shep with
his flabby arms. Then there was movement at the other side,
and as Shep turned a fist flashed from the gaslights and hit
him between the eyes. As he fell, he saw Dennis watching
him grimly.

Then a high, nasal voice was crying, ". . . thirteen . . . fourteen . . . !" He raised his head. Across the ring, Charlie Dennis was smoking a cigar, his heavy white arms lying along
the ropes. Two men in shirtsleeves and derbies were dragging
out the first man who had been knocked down. Another
timekeeper finished his count and John Allan, the pride of
Globe, was hauled under the ropes. The shouting and
carbide-glare were part of a nightmare Shep was having.

". . . Forty-five, forty-six!"

A hand was pumping up and down by his head. The earth
yielded a fragrance that somehow bucked him up. Suddenly
he was filled with an urge to rise. His mind cleared, he got
onto all fours, breathed deeply for a moment, and stood up.

Dennis rushed across the ground, swung hard at his head
and blinked when he saw that Shep had bounced out of reach.
Shep slipped in to smash him on the chin. Dennis faltered, his
knees loosened, and there was a moment of shock in the
street. Then the superintendent swore and waded after him
with his chin on his chest and both fists slashing.

Shep kept moving. Now it was better. Having hurt Dennis
once, he knew it could be done. On the edge of his vision he

saw them dragging out the third man. Dennis leaped in with a murderous roundhouse swing. Shep let the big fist whistle over his head. Then he smashed Dennis on the neck beside the Adam's apple. Dennis dropped as though paralyzed.

All the sounds had gone from this street like water down a drain. Up on the wagon, Tom Haines was on his feet, staring down at the big, loose frame on the earth. Keeley looked startled; but pleasure invaded the gaunt face and he yelled:

"Come on Fletch—let's have the count!"

Fletcher Henry brazenly threw a bucket of water on Dennis; then he signaled a timekeeper. The count began. Dennis had now been down for fifteen seconds. The water brought him to his knees, dazed and glistening under the gaslights. A man reached in to slap his cheek.

"Charlie! Charlie, boy!" he pleaded. Dennis rose wearily. His eyes looked filmy and he did not raise his arms until Shep began to crowd him.

One of Dennis's eyes was swelling shut. The big torso was blotched with mud. He frowned like a man chewing a pencil-stub over a hard problem. *He is soft*, thought Shep, knowing he had not hit him that hard. He feinted at Dennis's belly, and the superintendent grunted and dropped his guard. Shep banged a hard blow to his chin. Dennis floundered back and got caught with another to the eye. He missed a counterpunch by six inches. Shep drove a straight one to his jaw and Dennis went down again.

Before the timekeeper could start, he was up again, white and bloody. Yet under the blood and caked mud burned the same cold, murderous purpose he had brought to the battle. There was no use suggesting that he quit. Shep kept flicking his fist at his head until he raised both hands to cover his face; then he went in with a short, hard punch to the soft apex of his belly, below the ribs. He stepped away to let him fall.

The counting dawdled. In the silent street there were little escape-valve bursts of excitement. Shep smelled the raw ammonia Fletch Henry had poured on the ground under the superintendent's nose. Another bucket of water splashed on the man.

"Slack off, boys!" Johnny Keeley called. "You'll drown him."

The referee knelt by him, rose and glanced queerly at Shep. He removed his derby and announced gruffly, "Well, boys, I reckon—reckon the fight's over."

Shep went over to look at Dennis. He did not think he had hit him hard enough to cause a concussion, but it was possible. He peered into the one visible eye, and frowned. Something odd about it. He shaded it; let the light hit it again; shaded it once more. The pupil was unaffected.

"He's all right," he told Henry. "Get him up to his boarding-house and have a doctor look at him. I think the whisky was what really licked him."

Tom Haines, smiling wryly, offered his hand when he went back to the wagon for his shirt. Shep took the shirt but ignored the hand.

"No hard feelings here," Haines assured him. "It was a good, clean scrap."

"Thanks," Shep said. "Let me know sometime when you're going to barbecue a Christian for your friends."

Haines did not like the remark. His face sobered. "Keeley will pay you off," he said, and turned away.

The gambler came up as Shep was washing at a horse-trough. He slipped a roll of bills in his pocket and started to talk about the fight.

"What was in that whisky?" Shep asked.

Keeley's gaze dropped. "Maybe some little pieces of cork. How should I know?"

"Or some little pieces of knockout drops that you put in it? Dennis was doped."

"You ain't going to scold me for that, are you?" Keeley asked sadly.

Shep gripped his arm. "You damned fool! He'll know when he comes to that something happened to him. Where'd you get the stuff?"

Keeley smiled broadly. "You'd never guess, so I'll tell you. Miss Jessie gave it to me. She said it was good-luck powder. She said that if Dennis drank it, it would bring you good luck. I guess she didn't want him marking you up.''

Shep blinked. He took the money Keeley had given him and tucked it into the gunman's shirt pocket. ''Give it back to Haines. And keep your mouth shut about Jessie—whether it's true or not.''

8

SHEPLEY WAS BATCHING in an old saloon in Hornitos, the soundest building in town. When he awoke the next morning his mind held an impression of something agreeable, a kind of indefinite glow. It came to him quickly: walking Dru home from the train last night.

As he carried her parcels, she had little to say. Naturally she had heard of his beating Charlie Dennis, and there were marks on his own face to show that he'd been brawling. As they reached the little house at the far end of the ghost-town, he set her parcels on the low stone wall.

"Well, so you're off on the great rainbow chase tomorrow!" she said.

"I'm already started. I found one end of it in the Miner's and Stockmen's Bank today."

"Nail it down then. For a miner's not likely to hold onto it long."

"I told you I was just a schoolboy on vacation."

"'Once a miner, always a miner,'" quoted Dru.

Shep felt bound to jostle her out of her intolerance. He said with feigned solemnity, "Oh, I count on the tommyknockers to keep me out of mischief. You won't turn them against me, will you? You put their blessing on me this morning, you know."

There was an instant of displeased silence. "Don't you believe in the little people?"

"Do you?"

"Certainly! Who do you think tightens the stulls and timbers to save the miners' lives, if not the tommyknockers! Why, you can actually hear their little hammers tapping!"

"Have you heard them?" he asked seriously.

"Of course not!" she said, exasperated. "Women don't go into the mines. It's bad luck. But it's true. Prove to me there aren't such things!"

"If a thing exists," he said, shrugging, "you can see it."

"Like the wind?"

"You can see the wind by its effects. It's stirring your hair, for instance." Reaching out, he touched it. It was silken, warm, and exciting.

Dru tucked in the loose golden strands. "Never mind that," she rebuked him. "Anyway, that's different. Take—take love. You've never seen love, have you? But it's there."

"Oh, I believe in love, all right!" he assured her, gazing intensely into her eyes.

She ignored the challenge. "Well, if you believe in love, why can't you believe in a bigger kind of love, which creates a race of little people to take care of the miners?"

Feeling guilty now, Shep pushed a rock with his toe. He knew they had to believe in something, these Cornish-women, whose men lived so close to death all their lives. "Maybe there's such a thing as knowing too much, but not enough," he confessed. "I can't take much stock in your tommyknockers; but on the other hand I can't offer you anything better."

"Well, if you don't believe in them, you'd better not go into the mines!" she warned. "You'll be going in with no protection at all."

"Not if you intercede for me. They'll always listen to a Cousin Jennie."

"And why should I intercede for you, when you don't believe in them?"

"Because I've fixed things up for Bill to work the tailings

all he wants," Shep told her with a smile.

"Oh—" she said, surprised. "Well, that's very nice," she added softly. "I'm grateful to you, Shep." And that nice smile came.

And now, in the warm morning, he decided the smile was what had done it. She was really a beautiful girl. In the moonlight her skin was petal-soft and tawny, but white on her throat. Or perhaps it was the fair skin that did it. He took her in his arms and she came, surprised but obedient. He kissed her gently on the mouth; then harder; harder still in his enthusiasm, until he felt her pushing at him. He had kissed her so long that they were both winded.

"The mauling isn't appreciated!" she gasped. "Was that what I owed you for the favor?"

"I didn't mean to maul you. I—I just—" He grinned and looked behind him. "I'll tell you what *I* think: a tommy-knocker pushed me!"

"They'd better not again, Mr. Freeman," the girl warned. "There isn't a miner living I'd let touch me. The man I fall in love with mustn't know a glory-hole from a pig-wallow. A miner may expect to find the end of the rainbow—but all his wife expects is to find the washtub eternally full of dirty overalls. And there'll be no miner's overalls in Drusilla Croft's washing!"

In the mountain-fragrant morning, Shep saddled and took the telegraph-road south through the hills to his claim. It was a fair road, built in the 'Seventies by the army during construction of a telegraph line. Warped and worm-eaten, the poles reeled along with most of the wire removed by settlers, prospectors and Indians needing a scrap of copper. On the scaly, dark-red hillsides were the mole-burrows and dumps of the mines. A half-mile beyond the last of them, he sighted his own diggings.

He tied the horse and looked over the tunnels driven by Haines's geologists. Donning his mine-cap, he fixed the carbide lamp and went in at the upper level. X-cuts had been made at intervals, feeling for the ore. Then there was a deep winze blasted out of the foot-wall where the vein dropped steeply. He knocked a piece of ore from the hanging-wall and tingled as he felt of it. It was heavy with silver. He had a vision Dru would have frowned at. A dream of prosperity he scarcely knew how to frame, since he had never experienced it. But it would involve carrying a checkbook, buying clothes for looks as well as utility, and courting someone in a fine turnout such as Jessie was driving yesterday. It might very well be Jessie herself in it, or it could be Dru.

As he walked toward the daylight, he heard team-bells, and leaving the dusty coolness of the mine he saw ten wagons drawn up on the slope. Farther down the road were blurs of dust where other wagons were approaching. He gazed in surprise at the crowd of miners. Many of there were sitting in what shade there was, while a gang of fifteen or twenty unloaded supplies. On the bed of a wagon stood Charlie Dennis, sleeves rolled, hat on the back of his head.

"Them four-by-twelves better be moved," he told a workman. "Leave some clearance for the wagons this time."

Then he turned and saw Shep. Gazing at him, he removed his hat and reset it over one eye. His face was patched with court plaster. He jumped from the wagon, took a short-handled sledge from a tool-box, and began knocking out the chocks from the tail-gate of a wagon. Shep walked over. He waved a hand at the throng of miners.

"What is this—a Grand Army of the Republic encampment?"

"Be another fifty along directly," Dennis said.

"What's the idea? Fifty would be too many."

"I only work here," said Dennis. Then in a quick pivot he seized the front of Shep's shirt and rammed him against the wagon, his hammer raised. His eyes were haggard and his swollen lip drew tight against his teeth.

"Now, you cheap, finagling mine-tramp!" he shouted. "I knew you for a fake the day I set eyes on you. But I didn't know you'd yellow out of a fight the way you did that one!"

Shep watched the veins swell in his temples. "Let me

guess, Charlie,'' he said: ''You were doped.''

"Ask Doc Wilson if I was doped! Ask Tom Haines what he does to partners who dope his men!''

"While you're at it, ask Johnny Keeley who doped you. When did I have a chance to dope you, if I'd wanted to?''

"I asked that question. When I came around last night, I went lookin' for Keeley. Keeley was out cold himself, but I found Haines. Haines told me the story he'd had from Keeley as he was goin' under: you made him a present of the whisky before the fight and told him to pass it around between rounds—and don't forget the fighters!''

"Keeley's a liar. He told me before the fight he was betting on me. He was just coppering his bet. Ask Fletch Henry how much he lost to Keeley.''

"I'll ask him,'' Dennis glowered. ''But you've still got yourself a date for a fair fight with Charlie Dennis. And there won't be any sixty-second knockdown rule next time. You'll fight till there ain't enough left of you to wire together. Now get out of my way. We're drivin' a couple of shafts today.'' He went back to loosening the tail-gate of the wagon.

Shep looked at the crowd of miners. Some were moving the lumber Dennis had ordered carried from where it had been laid down. Others were smoking in the shade and watching Shep and Dennis.

"Are you starting a mine, or setting up a soup-kitchen for out-of-work miners?'' Shep asked.

"Ah, now it's advice I'm getting!'' said the mine-boss, turning quickly.

"What are you going to do with this mob? I'd start by sending an even hundred of these men back to the hiring hall until we needed them.''

"Would you, now? But I like a man to be there when I need him—not twelve miles away in a hiring hall! So they'll stay here today and camp in Hornitos tonight.''

Shep looked at him. Dennis's taped-up mouth was smiling. ''You can't use over fifty of these men today. You've got bins and chutes and grizzlies to build, but the materials aren't here to build them. You've only got four tunnels to work in, and how many men can drill rock in each of them?"

Dennis smiled. "Like I said, I just work here. All my orders come from Travertine."

Shep's temper snapped. "Here's an order from twelve inches away: Start loading those men, or draw your time."

Dennis put a match in his mouth and chewed it while he shook his head. "As far as I'm concerned, you're just a forty-nine percent strawboss. Tom Haines gives me my orders. Want to tell me otherwise?" His battered face was keen with expectation.

Shep thought wearily: *Another brawl; the work stopped and nothing proved; and a hundred and fifty men camping on me.* He turned then and walked to his horse, cinched up and rode back to Dennis.

"All right, I'll bring the fifty-one-percent man, or a letter from him. Be prepared to drag your freight when you see me coming."

Passing the upper end of Hornitos, he could see Dru's mother behind their home, a small black-haired woman of tremendous energy. She was poking a paddle into a copper kettle of wash hung above a fire. But neither Dru nor Bill Croft was in sight, and he rode on into the deserted mining town. The road was lined with one-story adobe structures with warped wooden awnings. Decay had barely nibbled at the buildings so far. He tended his horse, took a coat from his quarters in the Cloverleaf Saloon and strode to the depot. No train would pass through today, but he would borrow the handcar and perhaps catch a ride back on a freight tonight.

As he rounded the station, he was puzzled to see Drusilla and her father searching the weeds below the loading-dock. He stopped by the handcar and watched them. The girl wore her sleeves rolled and her hair tied with a ribbon.

"Can you make a living that way?" he called.

Both straightened guiltily. Bill Croft hobbled toward him on his new peg-leg. Dru followed reluctantly, looking embarrassed. "The girl was bringin' me some more of my medicine," Croft explained. "But she lost it somewhere. We thought maybe she dropped it as she got off last night.''

"Probably she left it on the train. They'll keep it for you."

"Please God they will!" breathed Croft.

"I'm going down today," Shep told them. "Can I pick up some more for you?"

Dru shook her head. "It was a prescription—an old one. But you might ask at the depot whether I left a red tobacco can there. Though I think I must have lost it when the train stopped and everything went on the floor."

She was talking rapidly, but not meeting his eyes. *She remembers*, he thought. "Well, if it's a prescription, the drugstore will have it on file. Which store was it?"

"Don't trouble yourself!" said Croft sharply. Then he grinned sheepishly, exposing those wonderful gold teeth. "Excuse my bad temper. I'm a little put out with the girl. It's not a big thing, so I don't want you putting yourself out."

Shep levered the handcar onto the tracks. *One of these days*, he thought, *they're going to slip and tell me what they really do for a living*. Something about their work at the amalgamation mill was peculiar; something about his medicine which was important enough to search the weeds for, but not important enough to replace, piqued his curiosity. As he put his weight on the bar and glided down the tracks, they were searching the weeds again. Passing Dru, he called softly:

"It'll be a lonesome walk from the station tonight. Have a tommyknocker meet me, will you?"

She straightened, blushing and indignant. "If they listen to me, they'll never go near you. Not unless they fancy being mauled."

9

THE MORNING AFTER THE FIGHT, Tom Haines visited all the saloons and hangouts where Johnny Keeley spent his time, searching for Keeley with a mounting anger. But the gunman was holed up somewhere, waiting for Haines to cool off. Haines had lost five hundred dollars through Keeley's doping of Charlie Dennis. Finally Haines gave up. In due time Keeley would come whistling out of his hideout, sure of the rueful acceptance accorded a precocious child whose cleverness had momentarily lapped over into naughtiness.

Now, in the dusty afternoon, Haines was arranging furniture with his lawyer, Jake Lund, in the quarters he had rented across the street from the Two Nations Saloon. The painter had finished cementing the gilt legend on the window: *Arizona Mining & Milling Co*. The big man-high safe had been moved from Haines's Seven-Eleven headquarters and stood open and almost empty. The room was narrow and high, with pictures and framed stock certificates hung on the walls. Behind a tongue-and-groove barrier in front were the desks and cabinets.

At four o'clock, Lund announced, "I'll go read my mail and be back."

Haines growled something and the lawyer left. Tall and hard-eyed, Haines contemplated the street-traffic. The dam-

59

age Keeley had done reached beyond the money Haines had
lost. The whole idea of the fight was to start Freeman off in a
properly humble mood, against the day when he began to
protest the rapid draining-of of his assets. A whipped man
would make less fuss. But Keeley had handed him a cheap
victory, perhaps made even Dennis wonder whether Freeman
or the doped whisky had licked him.

At that moment a familiar figure emerged from the Two
Nations. Johnny Keeley stood for a moment leaning against
the enameled beer-shield beside the batwing doors, chewing
a matchstick. His yellow vest hung open, his Stetson rested
on the side of his head. He'd probably been drinking and
wenching all night on the money he had won on the fight,
Haines reflected sourly.

Keeley spat out the match, lazily hitched up his pearl-
handled Colt, and started across the street. Haines turned and
started inserting red pins into a wall map. He heard Keeley's
sauntering bootheels enter the office. He did not look around,
and presently the gambler chuckled.

"Well, looka here! Open for business, eh?"

He was coming toward Haines, as Haines watched his
reflection in the window. As he halted behind him, Tom
Haines pivoted. He saw Johnny Keeley's horsy features sag.
The heel of Haines's fist smashed into the base of the gambler's neck. The heavy-lidded eyes squeezed shut, and long-
shanked Johnny Keeley dropped to his knees. In an instant
Haines had his Colt and was holding it cocked on him, a lean
anger in his face.

"Yes, sir, we're wide open for business! But not your kind
of tinhorn business. This is the rest of the pot you won,
dealer!"

Keeley's face was the color of cement. He watched the
bright ring of the gun-muzzle. "What the hell, Tom!" he
gasped.

"That's what I said when I heard Dennis had been doped!
'What the hell! I thought that cheap cardsharp was on my
payroll.' "

Keeley winced as the gun clicked. "Get that gun off me for

a minute, Tom, and I'll tell you what happened."

"Oh, I know what happened! I lost my bankroll and the chance to soften Freeman."

"There's a roll in my hip-pocket," Keeley said huskily. "A thousand bucks. Half of it's yours—what you lost to Freeman."

Haines grunted. "I come higher than that, cousin. Let's have that story, or you're going to the pokey. Then it'll be back to Yuma for fixing a bet and attempting to poison Charlie Dennis. What about it? Did you dope him?"

Keeley raised one hand fervently. "Yes. But before God, Tom, somebody told me to!"

"Who? A little money-bird?"

Keeley steadied. "Your sister. You want me to tell them that up at the jail?"

A small chime sounded in Haines's head. Jessie! Yes, by God, it sounded like Jessie! The gun sagged. "When did this happen?"

"About five yesterday. She sent for me at the saloon. I was dealin' but I got somebody to spell me. She gave me a little package of stuff she said was good-luck powder. If I put it in Charlie's drink, it would bring Freeman good luck."

"And I suppose you didn't know what she was doing? She knew Dennis would maul him like a grizzly, in a fair fight. Why didn't you tell me?"

Keeley rose and dusted his knees. He took a fat roll of goldbacks from his hip pocket. "Well, she put it to me like this: Dennis wouldn't do things the way you wanted him to unless he had a grudge against Freeman. And that's so, Tom. Think about it. That thick-headed Mick would have got religion before we finished with Freeman, unless he was sore at him. Now he knows he was doped, but he thinks Freeman put me up to it!"

"You know why he thinks so?" Haines snorted. "Because when he came charging into the saloon last night looking for you, I told him so, to get him off our backs! Why'd you bet my money on him, if you knew he was going to lose?"

Keeley was peeling off twenty-dollar bills. "I'd already made the bet for you. If I tried to back out, how would we look? Here's your five hundred. I figure you're getting something worth more than the roll you'd 'a' won by Charlie winning."

Haines took the money; frowned at it and thought to himself as he folded it over, *That's Jessie talking, not Keeley. That's too smart for the dealer*.

Suddenly Keeley said, "Hey! Look yonder."

He was staring at a man coming up the walk from the foot of the street. It was Shep Freeman. His coat was over his shoulder, his hat low on his brow, as he strode up the road through the traffic of horses and buggies.

"Reckon him and Charlie had a lovers' quarrel?" grinned Keeley. "He looks to be on the prod."

Haines returned the revolver. "Don't ever pull one like that on me again," he warned. "I've got a long memory for doublecrosses. Now, keep your mouth shut while he's here. If he gets rough, I'll give you the sign to throw the fear into him."

Shep had almost passed the new office when he noticed the legend on the window. He halted to glance inside. Then he turned and went in. There was a pine smell from the new tongue-and-groove counter. His eyes roved the room, noting the maps and pictures on the walls, the big safe. His gaze stopped on Tom Haines, who was bending above a desk. Near by, Johnny Keeley was rolling a cagarette. Haines looked around and straightened.

"Hello! The winner and new champion, eh? How do we look? Thought we'd better let people know we're in business."

Shep gazed around the big, half-empty room. "Will we still be in business after we pay the rent on this hotel?"

Haines laughed. "If we can't pay office rent, we might as well quit anyway. Think big, Shep!"

Shep looked at Keeley. "Did you know this big thinker gave Dennis knockout drops last night?"

Keeley shaped his lips and blew a smoke-ring, then pushed

his cigarette through the center of it. "Is that any skin off your nose? If I hadn't, Dennis would have whipped the socks off you."

"He was ready to do it with a hammer this morning, because Haines told him I gave you the stuff to pour into him. But last night you told me somebody else put you up to it. Maybe you better pick a story and stay with it." He went through the counter-gate. Keeley's heavy-lidded eyes watched him carefully.

"Don't try to spare my feelings, Shep," Tom Haines said. "I know who doped him. Jessie and I had a little talk about it last night. But if Dennis thinks it was your idea, he didn't get it from me. I didn't name anybody. I just said somebody gave Johnny this bottle and told him to pass it around."

Haines's face was solemn as he made the lie, but Keeley gave a small, derisive grin. And Shep recalled what Charlie Dennis had said that night at the mill. *"Haines will pick your bones like you were a stewing hen."*

"Then let's put that in a letter for me to take to Dennis," he said. "Signed by both of you."

"What is this—a class in penmanship?" Haines complained. "I'll tell Charlie when I see him."

"Then you'd better see him today. He's take a Grand Army of shiftless miners up there to do the work of fifty men. I told him to fire a hundred of them, or quit. Dennis said he takes orders from you."

"He does."

"And he'll take them from me. Either he sends them back, or he goes back himself. Until we get bins and chutes built, we'll be paying that extra hundred miners just to camp on us."

"Look, mister," Haines said sharply, thumping on the desk with his fist, "I'm no miner or geologist myself, but I hire men who are. If Charlie says we need them, I'll back him up on it. Is there more waste in having to shut down to wait for men, or to have them standing by for a day or two?"

"A day or two? Ten days!"

Haines shrugged. "I'm still with Charlie."

Shep looked in blocked anger at Keeley, who was observing his frustration with enjoyment. Again he met Haines's now half-amused gaze.

"Put on your hat," he told him. "We're going up and talk to him. I want to hear you tell him again who doped him. Then I want him to explain to us why he needs that gang of miners sitting in the shade for two weeks."

Haines winked at Keeley. "Take Shep over and buy him a beer," he said. "Might sweeten his disposition."

Keeley raised his gunbelt an inch, sauntered over and took Shep by the elbow. "Maybe that's what both of us need."

"Run along," Shep told him. "The boss-man and I are going to have a talk."

Keeley's long, sallow face smiled. His hand tightened. "Aw, let's run along together."

Haines sat on the edge of the desk, his arms crossed, watching it. And Shep knew it was between him and Keeley, now. He glanced beyond him at the big, empty vault. "Is our contract in there?" he asked suddenly.

Haines sighed. "Yes. Sure. But it doesn't say anything about who pays for inter-office beers. I'll stand treat."

"It says something about hiring and firing," Shep pointed out, knocking Keeley's hand away and walking to the vault. He squatted to peer into the deep space below the drawers. He heard Keeley coming up behind him. As Keeley's hand fell on his shoulder, he turned to sink a short, rising blow into his belly. Keeley gasped and doubled over. Shep drove a crushing uppercut to his chin, and the gunman began to slide down. He caught him and swung his lanky body into the safe. He snatched his gun from the holster, threw it under the counter, and hoisted Keeley's boots after him into the vault. Then he slammed the door and spun the knob.

Haines was rushing across the floor toward him. "You damned fool!" he shouted. "If trouble's all you want—"

"A square deal is what I want. Evidently this is the wrong place for that."

Haines feinted a knee at his groin, and when Shep covered up he hammered a blow to the bridge of his nose. Shep

staggered back, blinded by tears. Haines was after him, fast
and businesslike, driving short, solid punches to his face and
body. In a deep place in his mind Shep was thinking, *What is
this?* while he knew he must fight back. But it was a lot to
grasp, that the man who had paid him twenty thousand
dollars so recently was strong-arming him now. He jarred
into a wall and heard a picture come crashing down. With one
arm raised, he wiped his eyes. He saw Tom Haines, white
teeth bared in his brown face, cocking his fist. Shep smashed
him with the back of his hand, making Haines miss.

Shep waited, his anger thin and hot in him, yet ready to
quit if Haines was. He heard a thumping and a faint yell
inside the vault. Haines came driving back, lithe and intent.
He japped at Shep's face and the blow landed skiddingly on
his brow. Backing, he collided against the wall. The wall
made his counterpunch more of a push than a swing. He stood
there, feinting, jabbing, waiting for Shep to try to duck away.
Shep feinted a kick at his shin, and when he flinched he
ripped a short, hard one to his belly.

He went in fast, smashing at Haines's face, clubbing him
with a hook to the ear. Some of the fire was leached out of the
tall man, and Shep cocked, measured, and hit him on the
neck. It was the blow that had dropped Charlie Dennis the
first time. Haines dropped to the floor, pulled his knees up
and huddled there. Shep watched him, breathing hard. But
when Haines moved again it was suddenly, driving straight
into his knees and pulling Shep down so fast that his head
struck the wall.

They wriggled among the boxes and pieces of furniture.

All at once the door slammed. Books began to land on
them, then articles from Haines's desk. They separated
quickly and rose. A black-haired girl in buttercup yellow
stood by the desk, hurling everything she could reach. It was
Jessie.

"Now, stop it!" she cried. "Throw one more, either of
you, and I'll go for the marshal!"

In the silence there could be heard the muffled voice of
John Keeley inside the safe. Jessie glanced about. "What in

the world is that?''

Haines leaned against the counter, breathing hard. ''My paymaster,'' he said. ''That's what the party's about. Our partner, here, slugged him and dumped him in the vault.''

Jessie gave Shep a quick smile. ''I can't think of a better place for a paymaster, can you? So close to the payroll. Tom, I said Shep wouldn't run away and hide when he found out. And now you know.''

10

SHEP CLEANED UP in a washroom in the rear. He could hear the Haineses talking, Jessie saying what she had to say in brief phrases, while Haines made dogmatic baritone replies.

"That'd accomplish a lot," Haines was saying as Shep returned. "Hurt me and you hurt yourself. Not that you could."

Jessie was standing with her arms crossed, gazing at him as he sat behind his desk. Seeing Shep, she said, "I hate to hurry off, Tom, but I don't think Shepley should be here when your paymaster comes out. And he'll suffocate if you don't let him out pretty soon."

Shep scooped his hat from the floor, his coat from the counter. Glaring across the room at him, Haines said, "I guess you found out what you came to. Dennis is still in charge."

"You'd go to war with your partner to protect a man who's robbing you?" Shep said.

Jessie took his arm. "Come on, Shep. It's a little fancier than that. I'll tell you about it."

"Think that over, Sis," said Haines, as they left.

"What's wrong with him—is he crazy?" Shep asked her, as they walked downstreet under the wooden awnings. The town was cooling, the sun gone now behind the harsh desert hills.

"He's just so ambitious he seems to be crazy. He's going to take the mine away from you."

Shep glanced quickly at the fragile olive profile. "Wait a minute," he said. "Is that what you were hinting at when you drove me up from the depot yesterday?"

"Yes. He can sweat you out in a month," she said sadly. "He's ordered enough supplies to last a year. He'll have so many planned setbacks that no ore will reach the mill until you've defaulted on a payment and he's bought you in."

Shep touched a feverish lump beside his eye. He saw at last the sense in what had been happening—the staged fight with Dennis, the hiring of a gambler-gunman for paymaster, Haines's stubborn support of Dennis. Yet even with the evidence in his hands, it was hard to believe that Haines thought he could freeze him out so easily.

"Does he think I can't afford a lawyer?" he asked.

"Lawyers can't help you now, Shep." Jessie shook her head. "He'll just be closing out a partner who can't keep up his share of the expenses. Is that illegal?"

"Does he think a man will sit still for a trimming like this?" he persisted. "If I can't fight him one way, I'll fight another."

She was silent as they walked on down to the foot of the street. They reached the strip of bleached grass before the depot. There were benches here and she dropped onto one of them and looked up at him with an expression of helpless misery.

"If you knew all this," Shep asked her, "why didn't you tell me?"

"I tried to! But I couldn't seem to do more than hint. I'm involved in this too, you know. Tom says we'll go broke if we don't make money, and fast—" She twisted a bracelet and looked up as if wanting to say something. He did not help her. "I've had some hard times, too," she said petulantly. "I couldn't go back to that kind of life."

"What kind of life?" Shep challenged.

"Don't tell me you haven't heard!" she exclaimed. "Tom and I worked as a team, taking money away from men who had no better sense than to gamble with it. I always reached a town ahead of him and found out who had the money. Once a man who lost some money found out Tom and I were working together. He came after me with a whip. Tom almost had to kill him.''

Of course he had heard the stories about the Haineses, but he'd paid little attention to them. True or not, they were no business of his, he had felt. But now he said, ''I've got a feeling that I probably owe you a horsewhipping too . . .''

''Because I made friends with you?''

''Isn't that the way the game worked? Friend first—chump later?''

''I'm not playing that game any more. I was friendly because I liked you.''

Shep smiled wryly. ''Now, there's a girl with a real warm heart. I guess you must have been kind of sweet on Charlie Dennis, too. So naturally you had Keeley give him knockout drops.''

Jessie's eyes filled. He could not tell whether she was acting or not. She took a wisp of a lace handkerchief from her handbag. ''I did it for you. Dennis might have killed you. He's jealous of your good luck.''

''But while you were saving me,'' Shep recalled, ''you had Keeley put a hundred dollars on my nose to win! You've got more contradictions than a mockingbird has imitations.''

Jessie dabbed at her nose. ''I did it to get back at Fletch Henry for the way he grins at me, as if he didn't—well, respect me. I had Keeley lay the bet with Fletch.''

Shep gazed solemnly at her. ''You must be wrong about him not respecting you. Why wouldn't he?''

''I'll slap you in a minute!'' Jessie said.

''What would a girl like you do for a man if she really loved him? It almost gives me gooseflesh.''

Jessie rose, exasperated. ''I'll tell you what she'd do: she'd advise him to take what he's got left and get out. Go back to medical school. Go into business. But if you stay here and try to fight, you'll wind up with nothing at all.''

''Fighting's what I'm going to do, though. There's something called conspiracy to defraud. With you as a witness, I could break that contract and sue for damages. I mean,'' he added, ''if you were willing to go that far to help me—''

''Where would you be then?'' she argued. ''You'd have to return the money, and you'd owe your lawyer. You still wouldn't have anything out of the mine, and the same thing might happen the next time you signed a contract with someone. Mining is a game for men with big money and no scruples, Shep. Whatever you think of Tom and me,'' she begged, ''think about yourself. You said you wanted to be a doctor. Well, you've got the money to become one, now, and finance yourself until you start making a living.''

''Will you testify for me?'' Shep asked.

''And be one witness against a dozen Tom could line up? He'd have all the bankers, lawyers, and engineers in southern Arizona to make fools of us.'' The greenish eyes scrutinized him. ''Do you really want to study medicine, Shep?''

''Why not?''

''Well, you asked what a girl like me would do for a man if she really loved him. She'd help him every way there is for a woman to help. She'd encourage him, and push him, and pull him until he got where he wanted to go. She'd marry him, if that's what he wanted.''

Looking at the pretty, intense features, he decided she really meant it. She could help cheat him one week, marry him the next. She was like cut-glass: every way you turned her you got another, flashing color. Despite himself, he smiled.

''In a mysterious sort of way, Jessie,'' he confessed, ''you're kind of sweet.''

''You see,'' she beamed, ''I've changed! Men used to say that in a sweet sort of way, I was kind of mysterious. I could be useful—you'd see. A clever wife is worth more than her keep. Do it, Shep!'' she urged. ''Let Tom have all the mine—and the worries and the bad reputation. We'll have more than he ever will.''

Shep thought it over, though there was really little to consider. ''I keep thinking,'' he said, ''that a man who's foolish enough to let himself get into a mess, but not man enough to fight back, wouldn't be much of a doctor either.''

"Can't he be realistic, as well as manly?"

"Yes. But after a certain point they begin to call it something else. So I think I'll look over the cards your brother's dealt me before I throw them in. Maybe he accidentally slipped me an ace.''

He entered Proto Brothers' general store just before closing time. The floor was so filled with open sacks of dried beans, peas, and green coffee that customers could hardly move about. Hardware was carried in the rear. A dapper little man with a sandy mustache was pulling on a coat before locking up.

"Help you?" he asked.

"I want to see some revolvers."

From a glass case the clerk laid out several models and wiped them with a cloth. The double-action police model is the best thing we've got. Thirty-eight caliber."

"I want something that'll take forty-forty-caliber rifle ammunition."

He looked over some others and chose a single-action gun with rosewood grips. He bought a holster and shell-belt and buckled the gun on. If felt so cumbersome that he wondered how men like Keeley ever got used to the bulk and heft of that clunk of steel on their thighs. He had very little idea what Keeley would do now, but no doubt he'd kill an unarmed man as quickly as an armed one.

Through the dust and smoke of dusk he hiked up the hill to the miners' hiring hall, where a large man in undershirt and pants was cleaning lamp-chimneys at a table littered with *Police Gazettes*. The clerk looked at Shep and slowly shook his head.

"Not a thing, friend. The last of the men they wanted went out this morning. Maybe they'll be hiring again in a couple of weeks.''

"They're hiring again right now. I'm Shep Freeman. Can you round me up fifty men by midnight?"

"Why, any time, Mr. Freeman, but—"

Shep made a pencil-mark beside the door at about the height of his head. "If you send me anybody shorter than that, I'll send him back. I'm hiring by the yard."

"You must be figurin' on some mighty tall tunnels, Mr. Freeman."

"I'll need some mighty tall miners before they ever get in the tunnels. I might as well tell you: Dennis and I apparently didn't finish our scrap in the ring last night. He's up there mining like he'd never seen ore before, and when I tried to straighten him out he got proddy. So I'm going up and show him who's boss. I'll have a flat-car at the depot at midnight. Can you load it for me?"

"Can I not!" grinned the clerk, reaching for a ledger. "And I'll start with Grady Galloway, who never had anything but cross words with Dennis in his life. That's why I couldn't send him this morning. Fifty tall miners at midnight: They'll be waiting, Mr. Freeman."

When he made arrangements at the depot for a flat-car and locomotive, he remembered his promise to ask about the tobacco can Dru had lost on the train. He asked the dispatcher, who found the old Mexican who swept out the station and the cars. They talked in Spanish.

"He says, yes, he found one," the dispatcher announced. "He threw the medicine out and took the can home. By now he's probably made it into a bathtub for his grandchildren."

"Ask him where he threw the medicine. I might be able to tell what it was."

There was some more conversation. "He says he threw it in the wash near his shack, across the line.

"So be it," Shep sighed. "Don't forget that car. I want to pull out at twelve sharp."

At nine-fifteen, Johnny Keeley, grimly roving the town like a stalker of game, came at last to the depot. Through a murky windowpane he saw Pete Carlin, the telegrapher, reading a newspaper beside his key. Moving silently, Keeley placed himself close to an open window. Through it he could

study the waiting-room. A water-stained clock on the wall
clinked noisily. A harp-lamp with a dirty chimney provided a
sickroom illumination, and Keeley saw that no one was
sitting on the varnished benches. A faint wash of light illumi-
nated Keeley's features, tight-lipped and gouged with
shadow, a swelling on his jaw. As he was about to leave the
window he discovered a man sleeping on a bench near the
baggage-counter with a newspaper over his face. Keeley's
mouth tightened. The hammer of his Colt went back without
a click. The sear had been filed off because Johnny was a
snap-shot artist. He studied the sleeper for a few moments,
saw the holes in his shoes and the hand dangling slackly near
the floor, a withered old hand with veins like blue, branching
roots under the skin. Keeley's lips formed a word and he
replaced the Colt.

He moved around to the waiting-bench facing the tracks.
"Take it easy, Johnny," Haines had kept saying. *"Man in
your business ought to know patience by now. Relax."*

Keeley knew patience. It was all that had brought him
through that second summer at Yuma. But Keeley also knew
rage and compulsion. This golden boy of the ghost-towns—
this Lucky Shep Freeman—had squandered a whole
lifetime's luck today when he hit Johnny Keeley. Keeley's
deepset eyes roved the tracks with drowsy ferocity. No one in
sight but a man inspecting the journals of a flat-car on a
siding. The gunman entered the station.

The telegrapher lowered his spectacles to peer at him.
"Howdy, Johnny. What's up?"

"Tom Haines is waitin' for that fella Freeman. Been
around?"

"His name's on the board." Carlin looked up at a
blackboard. "'One flat-car, twelve P.M.' So you can catch
him here around midnight, if you don't before."

"Where's he goin' with a flat-car?"

"To the Apache Hill concentrate mill."

"Mill's closed. What's he goin' there for?"

Shrugging, the telegrapher returned to his newspaper.
"Better find Freeman for that one. As far as I know there

won't be anything on the flat-car but Freeman. Maybe he just likes to stretch out when he travels."

Stretched out, thought Keeley, would be a mighty fine way for Freeman to travel.

He returned to Fletch Henry's saloon to see what he could learn. A number of miners in clean work-clothes were having drinks. Near the piano, a little glee-club of Cousin Jacks were signing in Old World harmony.

"What's all the caterwauling?" Keeley asked Henry, behind the bar.

The saloonkeeper regared him coolly and continued filling whisky glasses on a tray. Fletch had been far from cordial since losing to Keeley on the fight. "The boys are going to work."

"Where at?"

"Ask me no questions—" said Henry. "Freeman's hired 'em, that's all I know." He hurried away with the tray.

That's all anybody needed to know, Johnny thought happily. They were going to get off at Apache Hill, hike cross-country to the Sweet Betsy, Injun up on Charlie Dennis's crew and try to capture the mine. In his room off the balcony, Keeley took a graceful little saddle-gun from a closet, rubbed it to a blue-and-brown luster with a sock from under his bed, and began feeding shells into the magazine. The jackets were brass, fat with powder, but the slugs were very small and sharp. It was a poor caliber for game, since the slug lacked shocking-power, and a wounded buck might travel for miles; but a man wasn't meat and it mattered very little whether he traveled after he was hit or not.

With the gun across his knees, Keeley sat frowning at the floor, pondering the route he would take. Up the road to Hornitos, he decided, then, skirting the ghost-town, to a ridge above the mine. From there he could watch the mine as well as the back-country. There was only one flaw in the whole thing, not a serious one but of a nature to sadden lighthearted Johnny Keeley.

Freeman would never know what had hit him.

11

A HALF-HOUR OUT OF TRAVERTINE, the locomotive and flat-car switched onto the siding which led to the Apache Hill concentrate mill. At the padlocked mill, Freeman's fifty miners detrained. It was now one o'clock in the morning, the hills very quiet, cool and serene. The engine chuffed back into the night, and Shep lined the men up. Most of them were Cornishmen, and wore the Cousin Jack's varnished derby which served for a helmet, with a lump of clay fixed to the front to hold the candle.

"We got off here because it's two miles closer than if we went to Hornitos and hiked from there," Shep explained. "Did the man at the hiring hall tell you anything about the job?"

The big, middle-aged miner named Grady Galloway, whom the hiring-hall clerk had mentioned as no friend of Charlie Dennis's, spoke up. He was a heavy-shouldered Irishman with a country haircut, a country stride, and a number of wartlike growths on his face. "Yes, sir. A job's a job."

"Incidentally, this job pays time-and-a-half," Shep said. "We ought to be at the mine before light. Galloway, those crates in back are full of ax-helves and handles for sledgehammers. Open them and pass out one to a customer.

Then fall in behind me.''

Galloway opened the crates and the men got their weapons. As they started east along the trail, the Irishman declared:

''Now, this is how a mine should be worked! One partner for the super; one against. And two crews drawing pay to settle the matter! What's the caper after we run Dennis out!''

First we move enough supplies into the tunnels to take us through a siege if Dennis tries to stage one. Then we go to work.''

He had prospected this area during the spring. They hiked upward through the desert hills for a couple of hours. At last he halted them on a hillside. ''Take the weight off your feet,'' he said. ''The mine's just over the ridge. We'll wait for daylight.''

Some of the men slept on the ground, but most of them sat against trees and watched the stars fade, and the light grow across a plain, from beyond a chain of mountains like peaks pinched up out of wet clay. Just at daybreak, Shep stood up and stretched. Galloway went along the slope prodding the sleeping miners awake and collecting them.

''Now we're going over the ridge,'' Shep told them. ''After we cross, we'll be in Dennis's country. Go as quiet as you can until we hit the camp. Then go in yelling like Comanches. I'll hike up first and see if there're any lookouts. When I wave, come up.''

The new Colt flopped against his hip as he hiked. At the top he stopped in some small, scattered trees standing thin and rigid against the breeze. From here he gazed down the hillside. It was barely light on the bench, but he could see breakfast fires burning. Cool and steady, a breeze blew against his face. Far to the right were corrals for the draft animals and pit-mules. He ran his eye along the ridge in both directions, but saw no indication of guards. He turned back.

Just as he raised the ax-helve to signal he heard a clink of sound. He swerved behind a big screwbean mesquite and drew his Colt. He could hear the men coming up the slope, thinking he had signaled. The sound seemed to come from a jumble of rocks some distance east on the ridge. He looked for smoke, trampled earth, or anything to indicate that a man had spent the night waiting there. He saw nothing at all, and wondered if he had heard a sound from the camp. But while Galloway brought the miners up the slope, he continued to watch the rocks steadily.

Johnny Keeley could see him standing behind the tornillo brush. Freeman was plainly outlined in his sights, but the thick, rodlike branches might deflect a bullet. Lying behind the rocks, his legs outspread like the trails of a fieldpiece, Keeley heard the men coming up the hill, and an oath rose in his throat as he peered down at them.

No chance now, damn them. His horse was two hundred yards along the ridge, too far for a sure getaway. For in addition to escaping, the gunman wanted to be unobserved. He'd have to wait until the miners crossed the ridge and went down the hill. Maybe better at that, thought Keeley. For then hell would break loose with Dennis's gang when the shot was fired, and everybody would be too busy panicking to wonder where it had come from. Yes, that was better.

Meantime he watched Freeman to be sure he didn't come to investigate the sound he had heard, which had been the sound of the rifle-barrel against the rock. In case he did, it would have to be hit-and-run.

"That Dennis!" panted Galloway on the way down the slope. "The scum of Ireland! He was the one started the companies charging us for the candles we used last year!"

"Tell him about it with your ax-handle," Shep said. He decided the sound he had heard was from the camp. Dennis would not have expected reprisal to come so soon, if at all. Dennis, Haines, the whole gang, thought the cat was in the bag. They couldn't conceive of a small cat fighting back against expert competition like theirs. He halted again just above the camp. The place was still a disorganized pattern of tents, wagons, and supplies spreading along the bench. Smoke fumed about the breakfast fires, where cooks worked at sheet-iron grills. Rails had been run out from the mouths of the tunnels to the edge of the bench. Chutes and grizzlies would be built here to handle the ore. Most of the miners were eating on crates near the fires.

Galloway gripped his arm as two men walked from a tunnel directly beneath them. One of them was Charlie Dennis. The superintendent carried a short-handled geologist's hammer. The big, heavy-limbed man beside him carried a pick-ax. Dennis was tapping a piece of ore.

Shep passed his eye down the line of men waiting for his signal. Then he waved the ax-handle, shouted and started down the hill. He heard Galloway's falsetto war-cry. And the sudden yelling and tramping of boots cascaded upon the camp. Near the fires, miners were lurching to their feet. Dennis and the man beside him pivoted, Dennis's face absolutely blank. As he saw the men charging from the brush, he wheeled to bawl something at his men. Dropping plates and utensils, they scattered to find weapons. Dennis planted his feet wide, hoisted his hammer and waited, a grim colossus.

The safest method, Johnny Keeley decided, was to ride down to where he could shove home a good, solid shot and take off again. He untied his pony and rode down the hill, bearing east. His eye trailed the attackers as they drifted toward the mine-camp. Then he dismounted and anchored his horse behind a giant mesquite. The tree was as wide and big-boled as an old pecan tree. He placed himself behind the trunk with his shoulder against the alligator-hide bark, got purchase with his boots and raised the rifle. Freeman had stopped above the tunnels and was studying the camp through its dust and smoke. At his left was a big shambling Irishman with an ax-helve over his shoulder.

Keeley took his bead in the middle of Freeman's back. An excitement pulled through him like a satin cord. In his belly there rose a cold shakiness. He was ready to pull the trigger, but a queer buck-fever suddenly gripped him. Just then Freeman waved the ax-helve he carried. The men poured down the slope, yelling. There was an instant of paralysis in the mine-camp, then a babble of shouts, men were running like hawk-frightened chickens among the tents and piles of equipment.

The excitement released Keeley. He took a bead on Freeman as he led the miners down the hill. But he couldn't get a clear shot. He decided to wait: Freeman would be in plain sight after the fight started. Keeley moved down to some rocks and settled on one knee to wait.

As Shep led the miners into the camp, Dennis had been joined by a small force of men armed with shovels and scantlings. The big miner called Grady Galloway started for Dennis.

"Ah, you ugly scum!" he shouted. "Call me a thieving mine-rat this time, will you!"

Dennis grinned, his arm worked, and the geologist's hammer flew at Galloway's head. Galloway deflected it with his ax-helve, which splintered. Head-on, the two men crashed together. The tall Cousin Jack whom Dennis had called Willy Matteson waited with his eye on Shep, his pick-ax cocked for a swing. He had a head like a clay skull, hairless and gaunt, and long, powerful arms. Shep feinted a swing at his head, and the pick-ax came off Matteson's shoulder in a savage swoop. Shep ducked under the iron point, and slammed his ax-handle against Matteson's forearm. The pick-ax flew in the air and Matteson shouted with pain.

Something crashed against Shep's leg. He looked down to see Dennis and Galloway locked together on the ground, sledging at each other with their fists. Miners swarmed past them to clash with the superintendent's men. A pyramid of crates toppled thunderously and a cook hurled a huge skillet at the invaders.

Matteson's injured arm hung slackly, but he was lunging at Shep with his other arm cocked. Shep parried his swing and smashed his fist up under Matteson's chin. Matteson grunted but seemed unjurt. He cocked his fist again, but then it seemed to hit him all at once, and he moaned and put out his

hands like a man in a dark room. There was something in his
face, a look not of pain but of shock, which startled Shep.
The big miner toppled forward and Shep stepped aside.
Before Matteson struck the ground, there was a smashing
blast of sound from the hillside. The gunshot rolled and
echoed about the hills. Matteson fell flat and lay still. The
back of his shirt was dark with blood.

Shep turned to stare blankly up the hill. A gauze of smoke
trailed through the trees. He saw a glint of steel and threw
himself behind a crate. There was a lick of flame from some
rocks, a burst of smoke, a bullet ripped into the crate. Shep
drew his Colt and fired at the rocks. He saw the dirt fly. He
fired again, high this time. He could hear men yelling in fear
and anger behind him, and heard the fight still going on. Then
he saw movement in the mesquite trees and fired at a flash of
yellow. A moment later he heard a horse running.

Boots were approaching him from behind. He dropped the
Colt and twisted about. A miner was lunging at him with a
two-by-four. Shep seized the ax-handle he had discarded and
scrambled up. He was still seeing Matteson as he began to
fall, the numbed and broken look of him. He parried a swing
of the miner's scantling and swung at his ribs, felt the meaty
smack and the gasping for air as the man fell.

He looked around. The ground was almost clear. Most of
the excitement was at the edge of the bench, where Dennis's
men were fighting for toehold. Battles were going on among
the aisles of piled materials. Nearby, Dennis and Grady
Galloway were on their feet again, circling each other, but
Dennis's eyes, dark with accusation, were on Shep. Galloway swung at him and Dennis, too late, threw up his guard.
The blow crashed against his jaw. The powerful body
loosened, the massive shoulders sloped, and he went down.

Galloway turned, his shoulders heaving. Blood streamed
from a cut on the top of his head. ''What was the firin'?'' he
gasped.

''I don't know. Keep them moving toward the bench. I'm
going to follow him...''

• • •

High above him Shep could hear a horse loping toward the ridge. Soon he lost the sounds and knew the rider had crossed over. When he reached the top he was winded. Resting on one knee, he gazed down the south slope which slid off to the plain. He could hear the horse again, now far off. Among the small trees he finally saw the gunman, riding west toward Apache Hill. He could not be sure of the color of the horse, but he saw that the rider was wearing a yellow shirt or vest.

When he went back, Galloway was marshaling the work. There was dust on the Hornitos road. The Irishman had the miners moving stores of food into the tunnels. Shep walked to where Matteson's body lay. Galloway joined him.

"What about this one?" he muttered.

"I think it was Johnny Keeley up there. I had a fight with him yesterday, and maybe it was supposed to be me on the ground instead of Matteson. Did you see anything of Dennis before he left?"

Galloway wadded a bandanna against the cut on his head. "Yes, sir. He said, 'If that's how you want it, that's how it'll be.' The damned fool! He knew we didn't do the shooting."

"For his purposes," Shep said, "it was better to pretend he didn't know it. Now he can report to Tom Haines that we hit camp shooting."

12

DRU DOING NEEDLEWORK ON THE PORCH, saw the beaten miners drifting past all morning. The Crofts realized there had been a terrible fight, but they were wiser than to provoke trouble by asking about it. Besides, their own troubles hung draped on their spirits like crape. Still no trace of the lost leaching materials had turned up, nor had they had news from Shepley Freeman about whether the tobacco can had been found on the train.

Dru's needle went idle. Would Uncle Virgil really sell the process to Tom Haines if they failed him again? she wondered. She felt terribly guilty for having lost the materials. Now she heard her father's peg clumping across the parlor. Croft came from the house with a cup in his hand. He was red-faced and a bit bleary in the eye. He had been drinking stone-fences all morning—a Cornish invention of cider and whisky, unmatched for lifting the spirits. She plucked some floss from the drumtight linen in her frame.

"I'm going to talk to Uncle Virgil again," she began, but her father hissed:

"Hush! There's Charlie Dennis!"

The superintendent was shambling wearily along the road between two men. There was dried blood on the side of his face; one shirt-sleeve was torn away and he limped as he walked. Bill Croft began to chuckle.

"Where be goin'?" he called. "The mine's the other way."

Dennis's bloody face turned; he swayed but struck away a man's steadying hand. "That stope a mine?" he shouted. "That there's a grave, Croft! We just left one of your own countrymen there for burial—but he won't sleep alone. We'll be back!"

As Dennis rejoined the march, Croft laughed. "To sleep with him, Dennis?"

"Father!" Drusilla gasped. "He said a man's been killed!"

"When did Dennis ever tell the truth?" scoffed her father. "Don't let him scare you." Watching Dennis stagger along, he chuckled. But soon his good-humor died in a groan, and she knew he was thinking about his brother in Tintown, waiting grimly for the week's refinings....

"I'm going up to talk to Freeman," she said quickly. "He must have brought the stuff back with him. You'd think he'd have the kindness to send it down, wouldn't you?"

"Dream on," said Croft bitterly. "It's lost, girl."

"We don't know that."

"I know it. Unless we can scrape up enough money somewhere to make Virgil's half of a week's refinings. Now, there's an idea!" he exclaimed. "Maybe we can borrow it. How'll he know where it came from?"

Dru pointedly took the stoneware cup from his hand and threw out the liquor. "Uncle Virgil said it would be gold after this, not cash. I told you that. And it would take a month to collect that much gold by the old methods."

"So he did," Croft sighed. "So he did."

Dru walked up the dusty mountain road. When she reached the mine, she was challenged by a man who stepped from behind a pile of lumber with a shotgun. "Where to, miss?"

"I—I wanted to talk to Mr. Freeman," she faltered. "I'm Drusilla Croft." There was noise, dust, and activity everywhere; mules, workmen, and materials in a bustling confusion.

"Go ahead," the sentry grunted. "But stay out of the tunnels. We don't like women in the mine."

"You needn't warn a Cousin Jennie about the mines," sniffed Dru. She went on and asked another man to find Freeman for her. Presently he came from a tunnel wearing a borrowed derby with its candle burning feebly in the sunlight. His sleeves were rolled and his face was powdery with dust. Dru smiled and reached up to snuff out the candle.

"You're burning up the profits, Mr. Freeman," she warned.

"A small price to pay for company like yours," he said, and feeling the same unwelcome pleasure he had aroused when he kissed her, she spoke briskly.

"I won't keep you. I'm to tell you how glad we are that you're in operation, and to ask if you need an experienced man on the grizzly. Has one good leg, and another that's replaceable."

"Why isn't he up at the tailings? I told you it was fixed with Haines."

"Mother'd rather he didn't start until your trouble with Haines has been settled."

"He won't find things any more settled here, I'm afraid. A man was killed this morning, Dru."

She closed her eyes for a moment. "Dennis was telling the truth, then! We thought it was just to scare us."

"It was the truth, unless he said we did it. We went in with ax-helves, but there was somebody behind us on the slope. Willy Matteson's lying in one of the tunnels. I'll take him down as soon as the marshal comes up."

"I didn't know Haines would send Keeley to snipe at us."

"I hope others will take it as quietly as Willy Matteson. There'll be some who'll ask why Haines would hire his own men shot."

"I've got affidavits signed by Galloway and me, and a letter asking Marshal Wilks to come up."

"Marshal Wilks won't stir ten feet out of town—he's just the town marshal. And the county sheriff is at Nogales. A letter for Nogales has to go up to Tucson and back down to

Nogales. You'll have to wire him. Even so, it might be days before the man gets here.''

A team dragging a stone-boat left them standing in a suffocating cloud of dust. Dru coughed.

"Then I'll take Willy Matteson down myself,'' Shep said, "and do what I have to until he shows up.''

"And what would that be? Shoot somebody else, to get even?''

"No—lock somebody up so he can't do any more shooting. It was Keeley. I saw that yellow shirt of his. I can't swear to it, but it'll be up to the marshal to find out where he was this morning.''

"You'll find Marshal Wilks a fast man with a beer, but a slow man with an investigation,'' Dru predicted. "But I wish you luck. I only wish you had the good sense to quit while you're ahead.''

Shep didn't comment. He took a match from his pocket and removed his mine-hat as though to light the candle; she got the hint.

"I'm keeping you,'' she said. "I'll just ask one question and leave. Did you ask about my father's medicine yesterday?''

"They found it on the train and sent it back to the depot,'' he said. "The only trouble is—''

An immense relief went through her. "And you brought it with you?''

He seemed embarrassed at her glee. "That's what I was going to say: it's gone.''

"Gone!''

"They decided it must have belonged to some passenger they'd never see again, so the agent gave it to the old man who sweeps out. The man said he dumped the stuff in the wash— What is it?'' he asked quickly. "You're pale as wax. Here—sit on this crate. Now breathe deeply.''

Dru closed her eyes and breathed; her shock gave way to despair. His fingers were on her wrist, taking her pulse.

"Did you ever dream you were rich,'' she murmured, "and then you woke up—and your heels were still run-over—and the sun was coming through the same old flour-sack curtains? That's what just happened to me.''

"I usually dream about Cornish girls," he smiled.

"And girls who drive matched blacks? Those pills were something my father uses to rework the concentrates. He says it wrings the gold out of that old cement like water out of a sponge. And now it's over, because of me.''

"You've been dreaming, all right," he chuckled. "There never was that much gold in the ore.''

"I've seen him mix the solution, and I've seen him smelt out the gold. And now we can't get any more.''

He scoffed. "Of course you can. Is it money?''

"Not exactly—"

"It's either exactly money, or it isn't.''

"It isn't, then.'' She glanced at his hand on her wrist, brown and muscular, with dusty blond hairs. "Have you finished counting, doctor?''

He gave her wrist a pat and relinquished it. "You've got the pulse of a girl of fifteen," he approved. "But you have the bad judgment of a much younger girl than that. Stop being mysterious and tell me why you can't get any more of the stuff. If it's that good you can't just quit. Would a loan help?''

His warm sympathy made her ashamed. "A loan from a man I've acted a shrew to? I said that all the money you made would go to supply houses and miners, and you'd wind up with a burro and a pack-ax. Maybe my father could take your money—it's his business, and it would be on his conscience. I'll tell him you offered it. But I see you as a man who already has trouble enough, and more ahead. I don't mean that unkindly," she said quickly. "But what will happen about the man who was killed here?''

He did not reply for a moment. Then he said quietly: "We'll get that straightened out, too. Tell your father what I said about a loan.''

Walking back to Hornitos, she thought wistfully of his deep thoughtful eyes and his teasing smile. *I wonder if he meant it—about dreaming of me? Tosh!* she caught herself:

He's married already. Married to mining, and the hussy will leave him bitter and broke. He was like all the other good men who had taken mining to their hearts. Every nickel he made he would drop down the shaft of a mine. Every pulse-beat of love he ought to have spent on his wife and children he'd squander on that golden hussy. And in the end she'd run away from him, laughing. And like her father, limping along on a peg-leg, he would reach out and try to follow, but never, never catch up.

Her father, asleep in a chair, awoke and dry-washed his face vigorously. "Well? Did he have it?"

"It was found and lost again. The janitor threw it into the wash. But Mr. Freeman will loan you some money, if your pride will let you take it. If you get it in gold, you can smelt up the coins and make a slug to take to Uncle Virgil."

Croft thought about it. "As far as the pride goes, why shouldn't I take a loan from him? I put him in business, in a manner o'speakin'. But as far as the gold goes, there may not be that much in the whole town of Travertine. It's a 'dobe dollar town. And with everybody hoarding what gold there is, the bank may not let go of its own."

"Fiddlesticks. They'll have to."

"Then suppose you go down with Freeman and tell Brickwood that. He'll be quicker to do a favor for somebody in skirts than he will me."

She was about to refuse, but recalled that if she hadn't lost the stuff, there would have been no trouble in the first place. So she agreed.

13

LATE THAT AFTERNOON Charlie Dennis arrived in Travertine with a wagon-load of injured miners. He marched them to Dr. Wilson's home, spoke to the doctor, and wearily hiked up the hill to his boarding-house. In his stifling, heated room, he stripped off his shirt, had a drink of whisky and lay down to rest. He had a vicious headache, and an emptiness where his self-confidence should have been. Mice were running in the attic of his mind, and would not let him rest. The mine-cough which always troubled him when he lay down ran its small, tickling fingers into his throat, and he reached for the Mexican cough syrup he kept by his bed. It was the equal, dram for dram, of chloroform, grain alcohol and corrosive sublimate, and seared the membranes so that they lay quiet and let a man sleep.

Presently he heard footfalls on the railed gallery which girdled the boarding house, and he knew them for Tom Haines's. "Charlie?" said Haines gruffly through the door.

"It ain't locked," growled Dennis.

Entering, Haines closed the door and looked at his superintendent as he sat up on the edge of the cot. Dennis saw his eyes running over the shelf of patent medicines and the Colt .45 lying on the floor by the head of the bed. The forty-five was for his health as much as the medicines, for Dennis was aware that he was not beloved by his men. He'd been shot at; explosions tended to go off irregularly. It was the price of extracting honest work from lazy men. But he hadn't worked in a mine where there was murder done before.

Haines had never been in this room, and Dennis, embarrassed and resentful, saw him glance at his drafting board standing against the wall and the shelf of self-improvement books—books on engineering, mathematics, geology—Bowlus on *Stresses; Speak & Write Correct English Without Study or Effort*—and all of them cobwebbed with dust and discouragement.

At last Haines sat on the edge of the single chair and stared at him. Haines looked grave and well-groomed. He brought an odor of witch-hazel and whisky.

"Where'd you leave the men?" he asked.

"At Hornitos, most of them. Brought down the ones that needed a doctor."

"What about Matteson?" Haines began shaking a pair of dice in his hand. By his question, Dennis knew he had heard about Willy Matteson's death; he was relieved at not having to tell him.

"Matteson didn't need no doctor. Thought I'd let Freeman figure out what to do with him, being as he killed him."

Haines's eyes whetted. "Is that for sure? The men told me there was a shot from the trees."

"There was. You don't think one of my men fired it, do you? When I looked around and seen Freeman, he was holding a Colt."

"Did he fire into the trees?"

Dennis sat up and vigorously massaged his scalp. "Yes, but I figured it was a cover-up. He just pretended to be shooting at somebody—like it was one of our boys."

"Probably it was—Charlie, what the devil happened?" Haines barked.

"We got bushwhacked! What the hell'd you think?" Dennis was surprised at his own brashness, yet unwilling to retract it.

"Why weren't guards set?"

"What kind of mining is it when you have to set guards before you can go to work?"

In Haines's hand the dice rattled like cracked ice. The strong, gray-eyed face was beginning to get hard. "Did I say it was going to be an ice-cream social? What's the matter with you? Afraid of him?"

Dennis rolled his feet and smashed his fist against his palm. "No, I ain't afraid of him! He just got me off-balance..."

"It kind of gets me off-balance, too. I suppose I'd better get a new super and try to get back on-balance."

"Get one, then! Get one that'll agree to run your company into the ground and make it look like honest confusion. But I ain't that confused. I don't mind a scrap, but I don't like fighting a man that's probably right. I don't know—maybe I'd 'a' hired riflemen too, if I'd been him."

"So that's it." Rising, Haines put a sarcastic stare on him. "Why not go into some nice, clean line of work, Charlie, like the ministry?"

"I'm no saint. But the trade will look at me and say, 'Look at Dennis—fleecing a greenhorn! And getting his own men shot up!' I don't need that kind of advertising."

"You're getting old," said Haines drily. "Your brain is setting like cement. Your methods were good enough for your grandfather, and they're good enough for you. Isn't it possible, though, that someone might come along with a new idea once in a while?"

"Like hiring men to soldier on company pay?" Dennis's bloodshot eyes accused the other man.

"Like taking out the ore faster than anybody ever took it out before," said Haines. "Drilling, blasting, mucking out in half the time its supposed to be possible."

"You can't muck out until the rock-dust clears," retorted Dennis. "I'll get the work out of the men, but I won't poison their lungs."

"Nobody's asking you to poison them," Haines snapped. "I've got four of the biggest steam-driven mine-blowers you ever saw coming down from Globe. Then I'm switching to water-drills to make that part of the work go faster and control the dust. The ore is going to move out of those tunnels like a landslide. Does that sound like mining that would get you a bad name?''

Doubt dropped like a seed into Dennis's mind. ''And you'll be milling this ore as it moves?''

Staring at the mine-boss, Haines said harshly: ''I don't usually clear everything with my employees. But for your peace of mind, here's some third-grade arithmetic for you: Silver is worth what they're paying for it at the time you sell it. When the Free-Silverites take Congress next fall, the price of silver will double. So I'll refine no more ore now than I need to to pay expenses.''

Dennis moved about the creaking floor. ''Well, it all figures . . .'' he muttered. ''I just had an idea—''

''That I was fleecing Freeman? He's welcome to go along for the ride, but not if he keeps on dragging his feet. The same goes for you.''

Dennis argued quickly: ''I ain't draggin' 'em! It's just that I—''

''You never did like the Sweet Betsy as a mine, did you?''

''Well, I was suspicious of it. I thought Bill Croft took too long making up his mind. He's an old-timer here. Maybe that mountain's sick, and he knows it.''

''Supersition,'' said Haines. ''Speaking of Croft, I had a letter from that brother of his in Tintown today . . .''

''The inventor?'' Dennis cocked an eyebrow. ''What's he invented now—a mustache-wax that'll peel off your zipper lip?''

Haines handed him a letter. Dennis carried it to the window for better light. When he had finished reading it, he looked up at Haines with an odd expression.

''Think there's anything to it?'' Haines asked. ''It sounds like he's raving. *'Guaranteed to yield three times as much gold per cubic yard as any other recovery process now in use'* ''

Charlie Dennis was remembering the night when he had caught Bill Croft poaching on the old tailings. He hesitated to tell about it because it would sound as though he had been holding out. Too, he had promised Croft to keep it quiet. But now he realized Croft had been making a fool of him by holding out on him. Just a poor miner scrounging out an existence eh? Whereas he was getting rich!

Pulling out a dresser drawer, he removed the little slug of refined gold. He offered it to Haines, who examined it, weighed it, and made a scratch on it with his stickpin.

"Where's it from?" he asked.

"From the tailings at your old Number Three mill. I caught Croft poaching there last week. Reckon I must've softened up for his girl's sake, because I told him to make arrangement with you and Freeman if he wanted to keep on. I kept the gold as evidence, in case he fell off the wagon."

Haines returned the letter to his pocket. "Probably no connection. Well, I'll talk to the old lunatic. If it's on a par with his other discoveries, it would probably cost two dollars to refine a dollar's worth of gold."

Dennis scratched his chest through the heavy underwear. "What about Freeman? What do you want me to do next?"

"Matteson was a widower, wasn't he?"

"Yes, sir."

"Then the widow won't be bothering us. So let's just let Willy be Freeman's problem—the hot potato he doesn't know how to drop. He'll probably send him down by wagon. In the meantime, I've wired the county sheriff to come over and make an investigation. Until he comes, we'll let Dr. Freeman call the squares."

Afterward, lying in the hot room, Dennis felt better. The battle between Freeman and Haines began to make sense. He felt sure that Haines was embarked on a gamble that might make mining history. If Freeman didn't like gambling, then he should have taken a preacher for a partner. The old eagerness began running through Dennis again, the readiness of a man who knew his trade and loved to work at it.

14

IN THE OFFICE OF THE Sweet Betsy mining company, Tom Haines cut the tip from a cigar and lighted it. Lamps were going on along the street. A piano tinkled in the saloon across the way. Putting his feet on the desk, Haines puffed on the cigar and gave his thoughts to his partner. How soon would Freeman come in, and in what frame of mind? Chastened—ready to take his licking and get out while he had something left? Or with his chin out still?

Wonder if he saw Johnny? he thought. For Haines was certain Keeley had been the sniper. Last night somebody had taken a horse from Haines's stable, at his home—somebody who didn't want to take his own horse from the livery stable and be checked back in. Soon Johnny would come sauntering in with his slow toothpick and slow grin, and deny everything. And as Haines thought this, he saw him turning into the door.

Keeley hung in the doorway a moment, peering into the dusky room. Seeing Haines finally, he drawled: "Whatcha doin' back there, Tom—spinnin' a web? Maybe I better loan you a match."

Haines lighted the student lamp and the green shade glowed. "Come here. Let me look at you," he said.

The light kindled on the gunman's almost fluffy golden

sideburns as he moved forward. His waxy, consumptive face was unshaven and creased with fatigue. "What's so special about me?"

"That's what I'm wondering. Somebody shot a friend of mine."

"Be damned!" said Keeley. "Who's that?"

"Willy Matteson was shot this morning. You smell like sage and horse-sweat, Johnny. Been riding in the hills?"

Keeley glanced down. The insides of his tight black trousers were damp from long riding. "I took a little ride down to Saltillo. Got an old girl friend there."

"What horse did you ride?"

"Borrowed yours," admitted Keeley. "Mine's paper-footed. Got shod too close."

Nettled, Haines snapped: "Between now and the time the county sheriff gets here, you'd better get that old girl friend of yours to sign an affidavit that you were with her last night. Because a lot of people are going to think you killed Matteson."

"Why should—?" Keeley began; but Haines slapped the desk with both palms.

"Cut the coy act, Johnny! As far as I'm concerned, they can hang you. I thought you'd be some use to me. Instead of helping, you break my orders to stay in town, steal my horse, and murder one of our own men! Why in God's name should I protect you?"

Keeley scowled. "I told you—"

"And now I'm telling you! What gun did you use? That fancy cannon with a cartridge like a cucumber and a slug like a pencil lead? They'll take a look at the hole in Matteson and start talking to people who own rifles with cute calibers. Or were you foxy, and got rid of it? But everybody knows you've got that gun, and the sheriff will want to know what happened to it. Then he'll start checking on horses. Am I supposed to lie for you about taking mine—and the fight you had with Freeman just before the shooting?"

Keeley, his cockiness gone but still truculent, rolled a spur against his boot. "You figure I ought to move across to

Tintown for a while?''

Haines grunted. "Not yet. The way it stands, Charlie Dennis is ready to swear it was Freeman or one of his men who shot him. He saw a gun in Freeman's hand, but it was a forty-five. He heard your rifle and figured it was somebody he'd staked out up there. It's a good thing Charlie's as thick-headed as you are," he added.

Keeley scowled. "It was me against fifty, Tom. I had to go easy. Don't do my best shooting in bad light, either.''

"I hope to tell you," grunted Haines. "Now, listen: Get shaved, change your clothes, clean your rifle if you still have it, and show up at the card table on time.''

Keeley winced. "I'll fall asleep in the slot.''

"Load up on coffee. Hike up to Cliff Garner's for the works before he closes the barber-shop." Haines saw him frowning at the rough slug of gold lying somewhat as a paper-weight atop Virgil Croft's letter. He was irritated with himself for not putting it away. "Well, move!" he expostulated.

"So here you are!" a girl's voice said. "The night-riding faro dealer of Travertine!"

Standing in the doorway, her hands on her hips, was Jessie. Keeley had turned in alarm at her voice, his hand seeking the pearl grips of his Colt.

"Oh—hello, Rabbit!" he said.

"Why, hello, Johnny—you old sharpshooter!" The girl came into the room and looked him over with furious eyes.

Haines spoke casually. "What's the trouble, Jessie?"

"I've just been hearing the gossip about Shep Freeman killing one of Dennis's miners. It just didn't sound like Shep, and I thought I'd see where Johnny spent the night. I thought if Johnny bungles his shooting the way he does his payroll-stealing, he might have shot at Shep and hit somebody else." Her eyes traveled the lanky body disdainfully. "And here he is smelling like a Pony Express rider and looking like he'd slept under a bridge! Tell me a true story, Johnny."

Keeley took her by the shoulders. "I'll tell you a true one,

honey: Anybody that claims I snipe from the brush is askin'
to get his neck broke—even if ain't any bigger than my
wrist.''

Jessie struck him with her handbag. She drew it back to hit
him again, but Keeley seized her wrist, and Haines lunged
around the desk and pried himself between them.

''Are you crazy? Johnny was doing an errand for me last
night. Across the line,'' he added. ''And I can prove it. So
shut up about him.''

''You'd better prove it, and right now.''

''There's a letter on my desk from a man down the valley,
offering me a share of a mine. I sent Johnny down to see
whether there was anything to it.''

''At night? Johnny? What kind of a geologist is he?'' She
walked past Haines and picked up the letter. The piece of
gold slipped onto the desk, and she scrutinized it curiously.
She had read the first lines of the letter before Haines could
snatch it from her. He slapped it face down on the desk, and
confronted Keeley.

''Will you get out of here?''

Rubbing his reddened cheek, Keeley said, ''I tell you,
the cats in this town ain't all mousers, Tom.'' He sauntered out.

''Well?'' Jessie asked.

''Well, what? If it'd been Johnny sniping at Freeman, he
wouldn't have missed.''

''I'll ask some questions about that errand he was doing for
you, Tom,'' she warned. ''If it's not true, I'm going to the
district attorney.''

''Save your strength. I've already wired Nogales.''

Jessie touched her hair, then opened her handbag.
''Pshaw. I broke my mirror on that creature.'' She glanced
past him into the shadowed rear of the office. ''Do you have a
washroom back there?''

He reached in his pocket for a match. ''I'll light the lamp
for you.''

''Never mind—just give me a match.''

In a moment she returned, her dark hair sleek. Haines

smiled wryly.

"Pretty, smart, and a hell of a nuisance. You want your cake to be all frosting, but they aren't baking them that way. You're holding a fair poker hand, Jess, but don't overplay it. Mining is still a man's game."

"And it's a man's world. But the women manage to survive."

Leaving the office, Jessie strolled downstreet to the depot. A dark wind, gritty with dust, swept up from Sonora. She sat on a bench until past time for her brother to have left. Then she returned to the center, crossing over to the alley which paralleled International Street. Holding her skirts above the ruts, she passed a line of trash-barrels, mops and brooms, the slatternly rear-guard of the street. Through a window she saw the desks and cabinets of the Sweet Betsy office silhouetted against the street. She tested the door she had unlatched while pretending to comb her hair. It had not been relocked, and she slipped inside.

The letter which had intrigued her so much was not in sight, and she bit her lip in vexation. But she knew Tom's methods fairly well. He would make a copy of it soon, if it was as important as the first few lines indicated. Moving to the letter-press, she found a volume lying beside it. *T.H., Personal,* was lettered on the spine. She opened it and turned the onion-skin pages until she came to a loose sheet halfway through the book. She moved to the window to read it.

Now, what do you think of that! She thought, in pleasant surprise.

The letter was signed by Virgil Croft. Croft had a reputation for balminess, but seemed to have some background in metallurgy, and might actually have stumbled onto something. If that was the case, it would be preposterous to let Tom hog it.

At McAlpin's livery stable, she told the groom: "I'll want the buggy in fifteen minutes, Paul." She was going to add, "Don't light the lamps," but realized it would put him to wondering, and she could simply extinguish them in the alley and relight them, well across the border. Maybe it was just a grimy little hook which Virgil Croft had baited and was dangling hopefully in the prosperous waters north of the border. But it wouldn't hurt to investigate.

15

IN TINTOWN, JESSIE STOPPED to inquire where Virgil Croft lived. Driving on, she pulled a *rebozo* over her head and followed a road along a dry wash winding south. She was pleased and excited. The letter from the old chemist to Tom spoke of something really important. Of course, Croft might not even talk to her. But at least she had a head start on Tom. And that was all she needed with any man; including, she hoped, an old rascal like Croft.

The lonely valley running down from Travertine tailed out on a plain. Here only a few distant lights dotted the dark brushland. With a throb of apprehension, she heard a horse on the road behind her. Taking a small pistol from under the seat, she laid it in her lap. Probably a Mexican cowboy, she reasoned—*vaqueros* always ran their horses. Or it might be Tom.

Following directions, she began looking for lights across the wash. At her left, some ruts took off through the sage. Beyond the riverbed she saw a faint gleam of candle-light. The horseman was quite close, now, and when she put the horses onto the turnoff she waited to see whether he would follow. She heard the rider curb his horse on the road. Then he was coming along the turn-off and plunging to a stop beside the buggy. It was Johnny Keeley. He sat grinning down with his trashy arrogance.

Howdy, Rabbit! You musta took a wrong turn somewheres, hey?''

"One of us did. Why did you follow me?"

"Shoot, I just come along to protect you. Seen you drive down the alley under my window without any lights, and I reckoned you might need a match. Takin' a big risk, Jessie. These here Mex are plumb hot-blooded animals.''

"Don't you know what's good for hot blood, Johnny?" Jessie said winsomely. "Cold blood." She moved the revolver into view.

Keeley scowled. "What do you take me for?"

"For as long as it takes me to get rid of you. Go away. I've got some personal business tonight.''

Keeley's foot moved from the stirrup as he pondered the gun. Then he gazed across the brush. "Ain't that Virgil Croft's patch over yonder? Bought a fightin' cock from him once.''

Jessie followed his stare, and something struck her wrist painfully and the gun flew from her hand. Keeley beamed as he pushed his boot-toe back into the stirrup. Jessie clutched her wrist.

"You—you girl-fighter!" she gasped.

"You start pullin' guns on me, Jessie, and you're plumb in my country.''

"What do you want?"

"Just to know what you're doin' here."

"Well, I won't tell you. Move your horse. I'm going back.''

Keeley reined over; but as she started to turn the buggy he said, "Okay! You win. If I go, will you give me a kiss—from the heart?''

"All right!" she gave in. She leaned toward him, her eyes closed. Keeley put the weight of one foot on the step-plate of the buggy, caught her with his free arm and drew her face to his. She smelled bay-rum, tobacco, and horse-sweat on him. He sighed and swung back.

"Now. Ain't that better'n fightin'?"

"Much better," she said crisply. "Good-night, Johnny."

As the buggy stopped in the yard, the light went out in the cabin and something was laid heavily across a wide mud sill. *"Quién es?"* called an old man's voice.

"Jessie Haines, Mr. Croft—sister to Tom."

"Did Haines show you my letter?" snarled Croft. "I told the fool to keep it to hisself!"

"Mr. Croft, there was an accident at the mine today. Tom had to go up at once. But he said it might be just as well if I came instead, so that people wouldn't be suspicious."

"He shouldn't have told you!" the old man repeated bitterly.

A luster of gentle reproof colored Jessie's voice. "Why, Mr. Croft! Don't you trust women any more than that? Tom and I have always worked together. He has no funds separate from our joint ones anyway. So I'm involved in this as much as he."

The gun-barrel scraped on the sill. "Are you alone?"

"Certainly! Do you think we'd want to share this with the whole territory?"

"I'll let you in," growled Croft.

In the dirt-floored cabin, there was nothing beautiful except Virgil Croft's bantam rooster, perched on a chair-back and watching her with one golden eye as she glanced about the room. Through thick spectacles, Croft's eyes darted furtively over her also. He wore overalls, Mexican sandals, and no shirt. The skin was loose and brown on his arms.

"How much will he pay?" he demanded suddenly.

Jessie smiled. "Aren't we going to talk first? I don't even know what it is you have to sell."

"Thought you read the letter."

"I did, but it only hints. How does your process differ from others? Are the materials expensive? Is the process difficult to control?"

"It's cheap, simple and three hundred percent effective. What's it worth?" His goggling eyes were coldly intent.

"May I sit down?" Croft flipped his hand at a chair, and

she sat at the scarred and greasy table. "We'd pay quite a bit. But we'd want absolute proof that the process is worth it."

"Your brother can bring me a load of concentrate. I'll treat it for him, give him the gold I get out, and he can think it over for three days. After that I mail letters to some other people. Start the bidding."

She had no idea where, at a time like this, she could raise anything. But she said boldly: "Ten thousand dollars."

Croft snorted. "A hundred!"

"Impossible! Maybe—maybe twenty. I'm not even sure we could raise that."

"You'd make a half-million the first year."

"*If* we had leases and mines. But if we tie up all our cash in the process, how will we buy them? What about a royalty basis, Mr. Croft? We'd give you a percentage of all we refine."

Croft chuckled to his bantam rooster. "The lady don't think we're very bright, Chucho. How much do you reckon they'd pay us after I gave them the formula?"

"But it would all be under contract! Signed, sealed—"

"And me delivered to the wolves! It'll be cash. Twenty-five thousand dollars—my final price. It'll be paid in this room, three days after I demonstrate it to you."

"I'll talk it over with Tom," Jessie promised. "Unless you hear from me, we'll bring a load of concentrate to you day after tomorrow. Good night, Mr. Croft."

Twenty-five thousand dollars! she thought, driving home. *Now, where could I get twenty-five thousand dollars?* Yet if the process was as good as he said, it would be worth hundreds of thousands. Then she remembered: Shep had twenty thousand in the bank! The other five thousand—well, there was always a way. She felt unreasonably, tinglingly happy. Not so much because she knew where most of the money could be raised, now, but because a partnership would be the first real bond between them. And if he still suspected she might have tricked him in the deal with Tom, he'd know better when the money began to roll in faster than he could spend it!

• • •

At noon the next day the alkali-streaked train pulled into the station and Shep Freeman stepped off. He glanced with care at the yellow depot and the street behind it, and then turned to assist the blond girl behind him from the coach. He was wearing the Colt he had bought the last time he came to town. It felt heavy and cumbersome at his hip.

Drusilla murmured a thank-you. When he rode through the village this morning Bill Croft had been waiting for him. He had said, "About that little matter of a loan—" and after it was arranged that Freeman would lend them sixty dollars Dru had appeared, dressed for the trip to town. He knew she was humiliated at having to borrow money from him.

He asked her to wait while he spoke to the baggagemaster. Inside, he asked the man: "Who does the undertaking here?"

"Fowley—the furniture man."

"There's one for him in the baggage-car. Will you send it up?"

"If you'll sign for the charges."

The tilted road was hot, and they stayed under the wooden awnings until they reached the bank on the corner. They entered the dark, grottolike room with its checkered linoleum floor and glints of brass in the cuspidors and tellers' wickets. It was so quiet that when the girl began timidly, "Would it be too—" her voice sounded so loud that everyone looked up. She started over in a whisper. "I'd like the money in gold, if you can manage it."

"In this town?" Shep said. "You'll probably have to take pesos, and like it. Two for a dollar, but just as good." He began writing a counter check.

"Gold twenty-peso pieces would be fine," she mentioned.

"I'll ask for gold, but you know how it is these days. Everybody's hoarding it, in case silver goes any lower."

He told the teller, "I'd like to see Brickwood." One matter was the gold; the other was that he had sent down a wagon-train of ore to the stamp-mill the bank owned at Apache Hill.

"Mr. Brickwood's gone home to lunch, Mr. Freeman."

"All right, I'll catch him later. Will you give me the sixty in gold?"

"Wish I could. The order is none goes out."

"For an old customer?"

"I might be able to get it, if it's important. Might, I say. But it would have to come from San Francisco."

Shep glanced back at Dru, who shook her head. He took the money in goldbacks. Outside, he gave it to her and she slipped it into her handbag with a glance up the walk. Shep laughed at her embarrassment.

"Don't be so proper. After all, your father gave me a lift into business."

"Into trouble, don't you mean?" Impulsively she put her hand on his arm. "Don't try to anything about Willy Matteson!" That's the sheriff's worry, not yours."

"It'll be mine if Keeley does any more sniping. He meant that bullet for me. I'm going to swear out a warrant for him right now, and try to talk the marshal into holding him for the sheriff."

"He won't. He's no daredevil, the marshal isn't."

"Then I'll make a citizen's arrest myself. I don't know whether I'd be in more danger tyring to arrest Keeley, or letting him run loose. He knows I'll testify against him, and he may be afraid I'll by-pass the courts and do some sniping of my own."

Dru shook her head impatiently. "So now you've found another trade as risky as mining—arresting gunmen. Are you afraid you might die naturally, if you don't go hunting Johnny Keeley? You needn't be: the mines will take care of that."

She walked off, and he smiled to himself as she went. He was sorry for her, because she had taken all the hard-luck miners in the world for her personal worry, so that sometimes she carried a sad anger where her joy should have been.

Shep walked a block up International Street to the city hall, a narrow, two-story building of gray stone. Small, arched windows and doors, and a tiny, useless balcony gave the building a look of coy pretention. At the end of a dark hall was the office of the town marshal. Shep found him with his feet on his desk, a very stout man wearing a black vest over a shirt with wide lavender stipes. A man with a red, wrinkled neck in a large and dirty collar sat against one wall working with a pen-knife at a splinter in his finger. He stopped work as Shep entered. At his desk the marshal looked up with yellowish, jaded eyes.

Shep introduced himself and Marshal Wilks shook hands but gazed at him with mild suspicion. "I expect you've heard about the trouble at the mine," Shep said.

The marshal flopped a hand. "Naturally. But that don't say I can *do* anything about it. What did you do about Matteson's body?"

"He's at Fowley's undertaking parlor."

"Well, I'll tell the coroner to look at him. But that's about all I can do for you."

"It's not for me. It's for the people who work for me. Suppose he comes back?"

"Suppose who comes back?" asked the man against the wall.

"The one I saw. I can't swear it was Johnny Keeley, but it looked like him. I'll swear out a complaint, at least. I've got some shells I found near the mine, and the prints of some boots are up there. And I saw him leave on a buckskin horse."

The marshal frowned. "Johnny ain't got a buckskin, has he, Jack?" he asked the red-necked man.

"Bay."

"I figured he wouldn't be riding his own anyway," Shep said. "Probably he borrowed one."

"What do you want me to do?" complained the marshal.

"Arrest him on suspicion of murder and hold him until the county sheriff arrives."

"Man, *I* can't do that!" The marshal's lips blew out as he exhaled. "That's Sheriff Walker's territory."

"Murder is anybody's territory, isn't it?"

"He don't want much, does he?" the marshal said to his

friend. "Why I can't touch Keeley, can I, Jack?...This is McRae—the court clerk," he added, for emphasis.

"You better not," McRae warned, with a graveyard grin.

"Suppose I make a citizen's arrest and bring him in. Will you hold him on my responsibility?"

Wilks scowled unhappily, as though things were getting out of hand despite his best efforts. "If I did, you'd be runnin' the risk of false arrest charges. You want to take that risk?"

"I figure I'm taking a bigger risk while he's around loose."

MaRae Spoke drily. "I'd say there was a certain amount of risk in arresting him, too."

"Let me get this straight," the marshal scowled, rubbing his nose. "One of Tom Haines's men was killed—but you want another of his men arrested for the shooting! Does that make sense?"

"It does when you were standing six inches from the man who got shot. Keeley was firing at me."

"Charlie Dennis signed an affidavit that you were flashing a sixgun around. How about that, mister?"

"And I took two or three shots at the man who killed Matteson. But the gun I was using was a forty-four, and the bullet that went through Matteson hardly left a pinhole."

Wilks closed his eyes and rubbed them. "I don't know. It's going to be quite a trick to arrest Keeley anyway, seeing as he went up to Hornitos this morning."

"What for?"

"Now, that's a good one for you to ask Keeley."

Jack McRae's raw-voiced chuckle sounded. Then there was silence in the office.

"Sorry to be such a nuisance," Shep said drily.

16

THE JEWELER BUFFED THE LODGE PIN and laid it on a black velvet cloth. A small nugget dangled from the Sons of St. George emblem. "Very nice," he murmured. "And a very thoughtful gift for a young lady to make her father. It was the father, wasn't it?" he smiled slyly.

Dru didn't meet his eye. "Yes." The nugget did not feel very heavy to be worth so much. A crime to melt it up for an old scoundrel like Uncle Virgil. But where else could she buy gold in this town?

"Your father hasn't been very active in the lodge lately. Not many of the Cousin Jacks have, these days. Things must be looking up, eh?"

"In a way. It's pure gold?"

"That's the way nature has always supplied nuggets in the past," smiled the jeweler.

"I—I don't like to haggle," said Dru, "but I can't pay more than seventy dollars for it. And that's more than I'd expected.

The jeweler sighed. "I'd just about come out even, miss."

Dru bit her lip and said nothing. Seventy dollars! You could furnish a house for seventy dollars.

"All right," the jeweler gave in. "I'll put it in a nice box for you."

As she left, the whistle of a locomotive sounded from the station at the foot of town. Gazing down-street, she could see it headed for the run into the mountains. She started walking hurriedly toward the depot. She could ride on the platform of the caboose as far as Hornitos. One more scar on her pride would scarcely be noticed, and while she stayed in this town she would be waiting, every moment, for a gunshot which would echo in her heart for the rest of her life.

Shep ate at a lunch-counter and returned to the bank. The teller said Mr. Brickwood was busy right now, but have a seat and Shep sat inside the enclosure and heard Brickwood's voice and a low, breathy young-woman's voice coming over the faded velour barrier behind which the banker had his office.

"You know, Carl, I could probably stop the whole show, if I wanted to," the girl said angrily. The Brickwood evidently made a cautionary gesture, because she lowered her voice. He knew it was Jessie before the door opened and she came out. She saw him rise, and stopped.

"Shep! Why didn't you send word you were in town?"

"Just hit the walk," he said.

Pleasure was spreading through her face. The dark eyes sparkled. "I want to see you right away. Will you be long? If not, I'll wait in the hotel dining room."

"I'll be right there."

The teller signaled Shep he could go in. Brickwood, searching through some papers, glanced up over his spectacles. "Right with you, son. There were some figures here...Well, don't matter. Why, about the milling," he said, beginning to straighten up the file. "Why don't we wait a bit on that? Till there's a good pile of ore for us to mill."

"There's a pretty good pile right now," Shep returned.

"But if the ore's cleaned up in two days, it won't be worth the bother of opening the mill, will it?"

"What if the ore keeps moving? You can't make money with a shut-down mill, can you?"

"No. Nor on a two-day-a-week basis." Brickwood began

flipping papers again.

"You won't find it in that file," Shep told him.

Brickwood glanced up. "Find what?"

"The guts to talk back to Haines. Did I miss him by much?"

"There's no call—" Brickwood began pompously.

"I wonder how the other stockholders in the mill would feel about this? They're losing money while it's closed, but here's the boss-man turning down what business there is."

A certain misery could be heard in Brickwood's voice. "If it was an ordinary situation, son, I'd mill your ore in a minute. But this is a case where you and Tom Haines might have a little trouble still. And I don't want to get caught in the middle."

"Get comfortable," Shep told him. "You're already there."

In the street, standing in black shade with the dry desert heat glaring off the road, he felt the bite of the pincers agains. Now he could mine the ore, but he could not mill it. He could try shipping it to Globe, but no doubt Haines could keep him from getting cars, or keep the cars from arriving. And if he went along with the ore, something would happen at the mine.

All right, but the hand that held the pincers would get tired before long. For Haines was punishing himself while he punished his partner. He remembered that Jessie was waiting for him. When he entered the hotel dining room it was almost empty. Near an open window, Jessie was intently adding figures on a sheet of paper. Shep reached the table before she looked up.

"How do you like my new dining room?" she asked. "I'm staying here now. Tom and I had a fight last night. I've moved out—for good. I'm going to have my own money, Shep—lots of it!" She cupped her hands, as thought to receive a shower of goldpieces.

"I should have your knack," Shep joked. "When *I* fought with Tom I didn't get a nickel out of it. How do you manage?"

"First," she explained, "you quarrel with him because Johnny Keeley tried to kill someone you like very much. Then you see a little bar of gold on a letter on his desk, and you get so interested you come back later to read the letter. After that you go to Tintown to talk to an old man named Virgil Croft— You've heard about it!" She stopped, dismayed, when he frowned.

"I may know something that ties into it. Go on."

She recounted the visit to Croft's cabin. "When I came back Tom was waiting. He was furious! Keeley had eavesdropped outside Croft's window and told Tom everything we'd said. So I moved out. And I won't go back. I'm going to get that process myself."

"What makes you think it's better than Croft's self-poisoning denture cement?" Shep asked.

"Because Dennis told Tom he'd caught Bill Croft poaching on some tailings near Hornitos, and apparently making a lot of money out of them. Now, how could he, with the old methods?"

"I wouldn't say it was a lot. Day wages, maybe."

"Well, there won't be any guesswork after tomorrow," Jessie said. "Keeley's up there gathering some concentrate samples. Croft will treat them for us tomorrow, and if it looks good enough, we've got three days to raise the twenty-five thousand dollars he wants. Brickwood's being stuffy about a loan, but I've already thought of where I can raise twenty thousand dollars. So that only leaves me five to make."

"Who's loaning you the twenty?" Shep asked seriously.

Her smile flashed. "Somebody told you. I'll give you a note promising fifty percent interest in six months. How's that?"

"What about the other five thousand?" Shep evaded.

"I have plans for that, too. Interested?"

"Puzzled. What do I do—just write off the mine and give the money to Croft?"

"Stop worrying about your old mine!" Jessie scolded. "What is it—just a mountain of earth with a little silver frosting. Shep, there's a million dollars in this! You've already got some leases, and before the process leaks out we could buy up lots of others.''

It smelled vaguely of something hatched at the roulette table. And he wondered where Dru and her father were left, now, for he was sure that Bill had been using the process. The pills—the moonshining—things at Mill Number Three began to figure. Jessie studied him, as if trying to anticipate his objections.

''Don't think you're going to make your fortune in the Sweet Betsy, because you're as good as finished there. Tom can't afford to let you stay in the game. If everything else fails—well, what do you think Keeley's on the payroll for?''

''He's going off it as soon as he gets back tonight.''

Jessie bit a knuckle thoughtfully. ''Don't be hasty about Johnny. He's not only dangerous, but he *could* be a very convenient source of money. If worse come to worst, he could probably come up with that five thousand dollars overnight. At a scandalous rate of interest, of course.''

''What could Keeley borrow five thousand dollars on? His Colts?''

Jessie colored faintly. ''That would be his problem. He gets the money somehow and we pay him twice as much six months later. He's made five thousand for the use of five thousand. And we've made a fortune.''

''But what makes you think he could raise it?''

Leaning forward, Jessie lowered her voice. ''Don't be a simpleton! Where would he borrow it? From Carl Brickwood, after hours—or perhaps from Fletch Henry. Fletch keeps at least that much in the safe and Johnny probably has access to it.''

He looked at her with amazement. ''Are you serious?''

She was blushing, but part of it was irritation. ''Of course I am. Isn't Brickwood helping Tom to rob you? And Fletch is—just trash. Anyway, Johnny could return it later.''

Inside that pretty head, Shep realized, was a set of values an Apache would be proud of. Yet running parallel to it was a naivete which prompted her to blurt out such a scheme without batting an eye.

"What if they catch Johnny in the bank, and he says, 'Jessie sent me.' Then what?"

"Then I say, 'Johnny's a paroled convict and a fool. I spurned his love and he's trying to get even.' You see, Shep, the rest of the world is armed with guns. Are you going to carry a slingshot? Maybe they don't teach it in business school, but it happens. Wealthy men have bragged to me of how they fleeced the public. Look out there on the street. There are five times as many people around here as there's a decent living for. So who gets the money? The one who steps up and says, 'That's mine.' Shep, dear," she argued, "it's not as though this were a new can-opener Croft's invented. It's the biggest thing in mining in a century! Just one quick stroke—and for the rest of our lives we'd never ask the price of anything we ever bought."

"In fact, maybe we wouldn't need anything but hard candy, smoking tobacco, and mail," Shep reminded her.

She sat back. "You mean you won't go in with me?"

"Not with Keeley in the deal. And not yet on any basis. All I know is I own part of a silver mine. And I'm going down now and hash out some details with my partner."

Jessie watched him rise, sighed, and a little smile rose to her lips. "You're so simple-minded. I wish I loved somebody else."

17

THE SWEET BETSY OFFICE WAS LOCKED when Shep tried the door. He turned to face the street, then. Some miners who had been walking up the street but watching him turned their heads quickly. He thought of Jake Lund's office, where he had signed the papers with Haines, but just then he saw a face above the red-and-blue paper pasted to the lower half of a window of the Two Nations Saloon—the white, pop-eyed face of Fletcher Henry, the saloonkeeper. Henry's face disappeared.

A ripple of uneasiness went over Shep. He wanted to touch the Colt at his side, to be sure it was there; but the movement would be flashed to whoever was waiting in the saloon.

He crossed the road, the sun scorching the back of his shirt. *They're watching me*, he thought; *they knew I'd come and they've been waiting*. Haines, Dennis, and who else? Was Keeley back and waiting to do that trick with a gun he did so well?—the only thing he did worth a damn, other than run a faro game.

He put his hand to push the door open; but thought then of the alley beside the saloon. He settled his Stetson, walked by the saloon, and started to turn into the alley, where brewery-drays squeezed through with rumbling kegs of beer. On second thought, he crossed the alley and continued down the street for the distance of two store-fronts, in case Fletch was still watching him. He came back and turned into the alley, walking along the deep, damp ruts to a mosquito-bar door just beyond a line of scarred oaken kegs. He tried it and found it unlatched. He entered quietly and heard laughter.

At a front table, where the light glowed though the imitation stained-glass, Haines sat in shirt-sleeves with Charlie Dennis and Jake Lund, his back to the window. A map was spread across the table, Fletch Henry was behind the bar in his long, tight apron, skimming suds from a schooner of beer. It was Henry who was doing the laughing. And it was Henry who first saw Shep standing at the far end of the bar, and he stopped laughing, cleared his throat, and said:

"Say, uh, Mr. Haines—"

Haines got the message. A pencil in his hand, he shot a look down the quiet room. Then he leaned back. His coat hung over the back of his chair; his white shirt would have been all the target a man could have asked. He stared at Shep for a moment with that startled question in his eyes. Dennis and the lawyer twisted around to peer at him. Shep started for the table. Haines began tapping his pencil on the scarred wood. Shep turned a chair, while they all stared at him.

"I hope this isn't bad luck," he said. "Taking a killer's seat?"

Haines's dark features were steady. "A riddle, boys," he said.

"Johnny Keeley. Is he still in the hills?"

Haines began rolling the map. "What do you want him for?"

Charlie Dennis's scarred face reddened. He had a courtplaster bandage on his forehead. "Don't you never get through looking for trouble?" he demanded, breathing through flared nostrils, like a riled stallion. "The last time I seen you, you was holding a gun. *Now* you come looking for the man that killed Willy Matteson! I'll tell you something: So are we!"

Shep sat down looked at him. "Matteson's body is at the undertaker's. The corner won't need strong glasses to tell you what kind of gun killed him. It wasn't a Colt."

"Don't tell *me*, damn it!—" roared Dennis. "I was there! I heard you shooting and I seen the man fall—" He stood up to stare down at Shep.

"Go have a beer," Haines snapped. "Give Charlie a beer, Fletch," he said.

Dennis stared at him in blank hostility. Then he opened and closed his fist twice and went to the bar.

"Now, what do you want?" Haines asked.

"I want to know what Keeley was doing at six o'clock yesterday morning."

"Sleeping, probably."

"Does he own a small-bore deer rifle?"

"Do you?"

"No. Keeley sleeps here, doesn't he? Let's go look in his room."

Jake Lund placed his long fingers together. "Let's get a search warrant first, chief." His bony face looked cold as tallow.

Haines slipped a string around the map. "And have Freeman claim we helped hide the evidence, Jake? Come on—let's take a look. Keep your seat, no use wearing yourself out on the stairs," he told Lund. "Got a key to Johnny's room, Fletch?" He caught the key Fletch tossed him.

Four rooms opened off the balcony. Haines unlocked a door at the right end. In the small, stuffy room, a green blind was drawn over the single window. The room had a cellarlike gloom. Everything important in it was located to the right of the door, which was hinged so that when it was opened only the portion of the room to the left was visible. The cot, a washstand, and a Mexican leather chair were placed so that a visitor had to walk past the door to see them; and in this manner Johnny Keeley could be sure of seeing him first. A stale odor of bedclothes, hair tonic, and tobacco permeated the air.

"There's his rifle," Haines said.

From a bracket above the bed he took a heavy-caliber saddle-gun with a blued frame and barrel. He handed it to

Shep, who put the tip of his little finger into the muzzle, looked at it, and ran his eye over the gun. A small brass plate the size of a nickel was inlaid in the stock, bearing the initials *L. L.* He handed it back.

"Cold trail. Tell him not to forget to give it back to L. L. when he's through with it," he said.

Haines glanced at the plate. "Second-hand, maybe."

"At least nobody can prove it isn't. I wonder if he's got any shells for it? Shall we look?"

Haines looked surprised, then annoyed. "Now we're getting into search-warrant country. Why don't you wait for the sheriff to ask the question?"

"Because Keeley may not be around by then."

"Then what are you going to do?" The caustic tone reminded him there was nothing he could do. Shep frowned in the cool malice of his eyes.

"Nothing—the same as you. What can either of us do? You've got me over a barrel with the ore, but I've got you over one at the mine. With a dozen men, I can hold it all winter. Maybe I'll go broke, but so will you."

To his surprise, Haines nodded. "Probably. I didn't want this ruckus in the first place. When you're ready to quit I am."

Shep was left with the initiative, and not sure what to do with it. In the stale, darkened bedroom they studied one another. "On what terms will you quit?" he asked skeptically.

Haines's face sharpened. "That we mine like we meant to stay in business—not scrounge along with a jackass, a pickax, and a wheelbarrow! Until you barged in, Dennis was getting set for the fastest start any mine ever had. I want to see that ore pouring in one end of the stamp-mill and the money pouring out the other. Would that suit you?"

He looked and sounded so indignantly reasonable; yet here they stood in the room of a man who had tried to murder Shep, perhaps on Haines's orders.

"That would suit me fine. Send Dennis up any time you want. I can work with him. But what about Keeley?"

"Keeley, Keeley!" retorted Haines. "Why in hell can't we leave Keeley for the sheriff?"

"I mean to. But let's leave him where the sheriff can find him."

"What are you going to do—make a citizen's arrest?" Scorn was deepening in Haines's face.

"I'm going to meet his train and talk it over with him."

"You damned fool! Is there a next of kin you want notified?"

"There's seventeen of them, scattered from Butte to Nevada City. All hard-up, and all waiting for me to make good and pay back what I borrowed to go into the tailings gamble. That's one big reason I've got to hang onto you like a deer-tick, and I don't want Keeley picking me off. What's this big business he's on in the hills? The same kind as before?"

"What kind was that?" asked Haines.

"Murder—is there a better name for it?" he asked.

Haines's lips Tightened as he swung the rifle-barrel at his head. Shep threw up an arm, and the gun struck his elbow. Then there was a flash which lighted the room, and a roar which hit ear-drums, face, and belly with a single enormous concussion. Across a suddenly open silence that followed, the bright sound of a ricocheting bullet slashed. Shep gripped stock and barrel of the gun in his hands and so did Haines, but neither struggled for it. Downstairs there was a crash of furniture, then boots on the stairway.

Haines's lips moved. His voice came distantly. "Why, that—that wooden-headed fool left it on full cock!"

Someone was in the doorway, asking plaintively: "What the hell, Tom!"

Haines's hands dropped. Shep held the gun. He wondered whether Haines had actually meant to fire at him. Fletch Henry, Jake Lund, and Charlie Dennis stared at them.

"Tom! You all right?" the lawyer asked.

"An accident—" said Haines gruffly. "We were looking at the damned thing and—any so-and-so that doesn't know better than to leave a gun cocked doesn't have the right to own one!''

He took it from Shep, turned, raised it by the barrel and smashed the stock against the mud windowsill. Throwing the frame and barrel on the floor, he looked at them. He grew calmer, having purged himself of some emotion that Shep could not read. ''If I don't roast his backsides tonight!''

''Somebody should,'' Shep said. ''If I see him first, I'll do it for you. Still feel like mining?'' he asked.

''Why not? I'll be up at the end of the week with the payroll and some ideas.''

''I'll be waiting.''

After he left, Dennis and the saloonkeeper drifted downstairs, leaving Haines alone with Lund. ''How about it?'' Lund wanted to know.

Haines pushed his hands into his pockets. ''I took a cut at him with it when he accused me of hiring Johnny to snipe at him. Keeley'd left the gun loaded and cocked.''

''Maybe he likes 'em that way. Was it Keeley's gun?''

''As far as I know.''

''You know, Tom, Keeley may cost more than he's worth. Where *was* he yesterday, for instance?''

Haines's glance slashed at him. ''Ask him, not me!''

''Well, if Walker starts asking questions, that'll be the first. After all, he's on your payroll.''

''He was temporarily off-duty—after the murder of one of my other men by parties unknown. Does it make sense to accuse another of my men of the murder?''

''Not to me,'' Lund conceded. ''Still, it won't hurt to talk to some of the boys who were there and get their affidavits. With a little encouragement, they'll probably remember quite a few of the things we want to hear, before the sheriff starts questioning them.''

Haines gave him a grin and a slap on the shoulder. ''Now you're talking like a lawyer!''

18

A MILE EAST OF TRAVERTINE, the railroad tracks passed through a fold of shaly, dun-colored hills and began to climb. Yellow grass grew in patches on the slopes, and the afternoon wind, rising from the south, hissed through the tornillo brush. The gaunt, gray framework of old mine structures stood among rusty ore-slides. Here and there a bin-and-feeder-chute crowded close to the tracks, where ore had been loaded into hopper cars during the boom days.

Shep rested in the black shade of one of these steep wooden slides with his hat under his head. A small coil of new rope lay near him. He thought about Jessie. It was amazing that she saw nothing wrong with letting Keeley rob a bank to raise a little cash for her! Yet in a way it had a certain jungle rightness: Brickwood was pushing other people around; all right, let Keeley push him! And re-membering where she came from, she was doing pretty well. She stuck in his mind, with her pert wistfulness, like a glowing after-image.

Above him the sky was richening to a deep blue, with some small birds swimming in the deep ocean of the sky. What a different breed was Jessie from Dru, he thought. The money Jessie would waste on a month's board for a carriage-horse would buy Drusilla a pair of blue ear-rings to set off her eyes, material for a dress, and some unaccustomed fanciness to go under the dress. But Dru walked in the traditions and superstitions of her people—hard-luck people who never expected to climb out of the tunnels. You had to learn to dream with your eyes open, dream the things you couldn't see. Otherwise you thought you had improved yourself when you doubled your dollar-a-day to two.

A bit of dust sifted from the weathered boards above his head. Then there was a trembling in the earth. He climbed the scaffolding, and dropped into the boxed-in, roofless slide which ended above the tracks. Up the line a whistle piped three high and breathless notes. He crouched, making a noose in the rose. Would it be flat-car, hopper, or gondola? Where would Keeley ride—up with the engine crew or in the caboose, if the train carried one?

He shifted the rope to his left hand, pressed his hand over his Colt, and listened to the chuffing of the engine. It was a small one, probably a yard-engine. Through cracks in the sides of the chute he could see the rails curving around the dusky hillside. The locomotive smoked into view, red-and-green lamps burning, headlamp still unlighted. Behind it was the tender, one hopper-car which appeared to be empty, and caboose. The head of the engineer craned out the window. Another man showed indistinctly at the opposite side of the cab.

Damn the caboose! It meant Keeley could be at either end of the train. It was traveling slowly, but too fast to jump for the grab-irons of the caboose. He would have to drop into the hopper and work from there. He hoped Keeley was not in the caboose and looking forward.

The scaffolding began to vibrate with the weight of the cars. A man's voice came through the clank and hiss of the loafing yard-engine. Then the shadow of coal-smoke darkened the chute, the heat of the boiler-jacket touched his face and a jumble of fizzing steam-pipes against crusted black-iron was passing before him. He had a flashing glimpse into the cab, as though a lens-cap had been whipped from the lens of a camera—the engineer gazing along the side of the locomotive, the fireman wiping gauges with a rag. Then the cab was gone, the tender was passing, and Shep jumped down into the hopper car.

He fell and rolled in a foot of earth at the bottom of it, rose quickly to his knees, and peered at the caboose. A few feet from him a spark traveled across the hopper, broke into smaller sparks against the iron side, and the odor of tobacco stung him. A shape rose from the floor of the hopper with desperate, collected swiftness. In the dusty half-light he saw a man standing with one hand extended for balance, the other raking toward his hip.

Keeley had his gunman's start. His left arm was extended for balance as the train rocked and clattered and the dust swirled up from the chalky concentrate in which he stood; his right hand was already traveling with the neat and certain movements it had learned—the hound leaping for the throat. The lanky face with the deep-shadowed eyes and high cheekbones was as frozen, sure and emotionless as his hand.

Shep blindly swung the coiled rope at his face as he clambered up, striking a vicious word from the wide slash-mouth. The hard plaits whipped the sallow skin. He drove in as Keeley's gun came from the holster, and locked his free hand on the gunman's wrist. The gun flashed. He felt the kick of it as the bullet struck iron and cried off. He held the thin, hard wrist and rammed his shoulder into Keeley's face. Keeley grunted and went back, working in silent rage to free his hand. Then the struggling ceased and Shep knew he was transferring the Colt to his left hand.

They lost footing and landed on the iron floor. Keeley slid away and rolled over to face him, lying on his side with his elbow propping him up. Shep smashed at the gun. The big flash blinded him, a cold, painless flame touching his cheek. He seized the barrel of the Colt, wrenched it free, and threw it over the side of the car. Keeley looked stunned. Shep dropped the rope. With both hands he went after this

tramp who had no trade but dealing cards and killing for
hire.

Keeley scrambled away, found a stone and hurled it at
him. Shep's hands caught Keeley's shirt and dragged him
close. In a hot fury he began chopping at his face, cutting
the skin over the sharp cheekbones and splitting his lip.
Keeley was clawing and squirming, but not fighting. In
Shep's hands he was as helpless as a woman. Shep threw
him against the iron wall of the car and held him there with
fast-chopping blows to the face and body. A man was
bawling at them from the cab of the locomotive. When
Keeley sagged, Shep straightened him with a roundhousing
uppercut, feeling a wicked joy at what he was doing, as
though generations of hammer-swinging, dust-breathing
Freemans who had bred these muscles into him with their
own lives were sharing in the victory of a hardrock man over
a gunman.

Abruptly the train slowed. Shep was thrown to the floor,
as was Keeley, a huddled heap on the bottom of the car.
Keeley did not stir. Shep sighed and blew out his breath. As
the train whistled, the station lights gliding past, he crawled
to where he had flung the rope. But the time the train
stopped, the gunman was tied.

Someone was running across the gravel. Shep heard a low,
urgent call: "Johnny! Hey!" He hoisted Keeley onto his
shoulder. "Johnny!" The voice came from the caboose,
now. From the other end of the train the fireman, clutching
a brakeman's bar, came clumping back over the heaped coal
in the tender. "What the devil—!"

"Give me a hand with this fellow," Shep snapped.

"Where'd you get on!" demanded the fireman. Reluctantly he reached down to help haul Keeley from the hopper-
car. At the window of the caboose appeared the face of the
man seeking Johnny Keeley. Seeing them, he was silent.

"This man's wanted at the marshal's office," Shep told
the fireman. "Go get me a hand-cart, will you?"

The fireman jumped down, conferred with some other
men, and eventually Shep heard a cart being brought up.

At the jail, Shep told the corpulent marshal: "Here he is. Look through his pockets before you lock him up, and see if the coroner can fit one of those needle-nosed cartridges he's still carrying into the hole in Willy Matteson."

19

BILL CROFT HAD CONSTRUCTED a small furnace in his back yard while Dru was in Travertine—and ovenlike arrangement of flat stones, a grate for coal, and a smith's bellows. Early the next morning he detached the nugget from the Sons of St. George emblem Dru had purchased, fastened the pin to his shirt, and deposited the nugget in a cupel for melting.

"Will it be enough?" Dru asked nervously. "Perhaps we should melt up the locket and chain I had from grandmother..." Her tone invited refusal, for she treasured the flimsy scraps of jewelry.

"All the gold in them things," her father reassured her, "wouldn't make you sneeze if you took it for snuff. It's ten carat, and little enough of that."

In a short time the nugget crumbled, flattening under a shining skin which soon coated itself with dross. With the blade of a pen-knife, the miner stirred it. "Brother o' mine," he chortled, "we'll see who has the cannier head in the Croft litter this time!"

But all at once he bent closer. He frowned and removed the cupel from the furnace with tongs. "What—what is it?" asked Dru breathlessly. Croft did not respond. As the metal cooled, he tapped out the little thimble of gold. With the knife, he made a deep slice in the side of it. And sat back.

"Dad?" faltered Drusilla.

"What jeweler did you say sold you this?"

"Lacey. isn't it—"

"It's lead, dear. Lead that's been washed with gold and given a little rough treatment to give it the look." Croft smiled, but tears swam into his eyes, tears of bitter self-mockery.

Slowly Dru stood up. Her face was grave. She spoke quietly. "All along, I've had the feeling that anything that came so dear, at the price of poaching, borrowing and stealing, wasn't worth the having. And now we know. Dad!" she cried, as he crouched by the fire. "What in heaven!"

Her father was pounding something on a rock with the hammer of the tongs. Bits of gold and porcelain glittered—wires and wedges of gold, tiny, gleaming shards of porcelain. Even so she did not comprehend, until he turned his face up. There was a caved-in look to his upper lip as he said:

"It was our last resort—my teeth. They'll make what we owe him and more. Tell your mother I'll want nothing but broth tonight," he sighed.

Dru felt shocked and ill. She went into the house without a word. Her father had pounded up his beautiful bridgework, with all the gold teeth he had been accumulating for thirty years. And that was what he was melting up to fool Uncle Virgil.

Later that afternoon, in a secluded arroyo a quarter-mile from his shack, Virgil Croft completed the test of his process. Jessie and Tom Haines had watched from the bank, twenty feet away. He would not permit them any closer.

"You'd better move if the fumes drift onto you," he said. "All the gold in Arizona wouldn't bring your lungs back if you breathed them fumes."

Haines's mind riffled through the list of chemicals he knew which gave off deadly fumes. But that was hopeless. Croft had had the leaching solution mixed and ready when they arrived with the wagon bearing the concentrate for treating. And he had dumped it on the sand after that part of the process was finished; then, while the smelting took place in four separate furnaces, he poured buckets of other chemicals over the sand and made it impossible to analyze even the leavings.

"A metallurgist can't be too careful these days, folks," he grinned.

When the process was finished, he produced four small buttons of gold. Haines watched him like a hawk, alert for trickery. On a Troy scale he had brought, Croft weighed each slug and scratched the weight on it. When he dropped them onto Haines's palm the gold was still warm from the furnace—obviously not something he had prepared earlier and produced with sleight-of-hand. Haines caught the scent of Jessie's perfume as she leaned close to scrutinize them, and his hand closed angrily. He wanted to slap some sense into her: barging into what was no business of hers— jeopardizing the whole thing!

"I think it's quite impressive, Tom, don't you?" she said excitedly.

Croft stood there shirtless in his overalls, his shrunken brown arms tough as alligator hide, grinning while his keen eyes goggled at them behind the scholarly pince-nez eyeglasses. Haines shrugged.

"Seems effective," he agreed with Jessie. "The big story will be whether Mr. Croft got out most of the gold the assays show was in it. The assays should be on my desk by now. Mr. Croft," he said, "just assuming the process is all you say, what's your lowest price?"

"Told your sister: Twenty-five thousand."

"That kind of money's hard to find."

"Not in the right places it ain't."

"It's hard anyplace, if you're talking about cash. I don't know why we couldn't work out a royalty arrangement—"

"I'm talking about cash!" Croft whipped out. There's plenty of big outfits got it if you haven't. But I don't trust them buzzards. That's why I'm giving you first crack at it."

"I appreciate it, sir," Haines said formally, his mind working. "Now, suppose I put ten thousand cash down—say three days from now—and pay you another ten in two weeks.

Two weeks later I'll give you another ten—thirty thousand in all. The extra five for your patience.''

''Suppose you shut your mouth about credit,'' Croft snarled. ''I'll take the ten thousand, all right, but if you don't produce the other fifteen a week after we sign papers, you're out your ten *and* the process.''

Haines's temper flashed, but he locked it behind a faint thoughtful frown. Croft's thin, raw-looking lips parted in anger. ''And don't think it's wrote down where any of your coyotes can find it!'' he added.

Haines laughed. ''What kind of operator do you think I am?'' he asked, hating the goatish old face and vicious mouth.

''I know what kind you are. You get a little purchase on a mining company, smooth-talk other stockholders into backing you, and vote yourself president of it. And draw salary while the company founders.''

''I'm surprised that you trust me enough to do business with me,'' Haines shrugged.

''I don't. That's why it's cash in the bucket!''

Jessie slipped her hand through Tom's arm. ''Tom's not so bad, Mr. Croft,'' she defended. ''People say those things because they're envious. But his companies are still solvent, where others have foundered. And this new mine is oozing silver, as your own brother says, like chicken-fat.''

''*What new mine*?'' scrowle Croft. ''That Sweet Betsy? Something wrong with that mine,'' he said darkly.

A cold draft went across the back of Haines's neck. ''There's nothing wrong with it that mining the ore in it won't cure.''

''Then why wasn't it worked in the old days? Oh, I know about the Triangle—where the cattleman wouldn't let 'em prospect—so this'n got overlooked. But they mined within a half-mile of it, didn't they? Look at all the old stopes. Oh, they prospected it, all right. but they were afraid of it.''

''Why?'' asked Jessie.

''Because the curse of the tommyknockers was on it!''

Haines's laugh bubbled up, but he held it, and then abruptly had no impulse to laugh at all, because the thought came: *Can anything this old lunatic says be true?* but he had seen the process work. Croft was a metallurgical wizard, if a bakebrain at everything else.

"Well, the Sweet Betsy's not your worry," he said. "All right," he sighed. "I'll be here Friday with the first ten thousand, if the assays warrant my buying the process. And I'll have the balance within a week."

Darkness swept in before they reached Travertine, and Haines lighted the lamps of the rented carryall. They had scarcely spoken by the time the wagon rattled into town. They were like two gamblers in a high-stakes game, laying their own traps, figuring their chances. But as Jessie stepped down at the hotel where she was staying, Haines said through his teeth:

"I suppose you're hoping to beat me to it, eh? Get the cash from Freeman or somewhere. Try it! Just stick your hand in the machinery again, and it'll be cut off."

Jessie said naively: "Goodness! Such violence!"

"You don't even know what violence is," said Haines. "Meddle again, and you'll find out—sister or not. I told you how they play this game. Don't make me show you."

He whipped the carryall around the corner to the livery barn, drove in and left it standing in the drafty aisle. He strode back to the office. The street-lamps were hazy in their gritty halos of dust. Something rustled under his feet as he entered, and he saw that the assay-reports had been pushed under the door. Haines drew the shades and lighted the lamp. Then he sat down to balance the assayer's estimate of what was in the concentrates with what Croft had actually recovered.

In an instant he looked up. The lines of strain in his face vanished; he grinned at the far, dim wall. Croft had squeezed more gold out of the stuff than the report said was in it. Again he bent over the desk, checking the figures, and at last he leaned back. His eyes exulted; he linked both hands behind his head and rocked in the chair.

But suddenly reality drenched him. *Hell, I haven't even*

got the money to buy the process, he realized. Brickwood would have to come through fast—or go to Yuma. On the other hand, what if he couldn't scrape up the cash without dipping into depositors' reserves? Bankers went to jail for that, too, and maybe he would simply dare Haines to do anything about that canceled check which proved bribery. So Brickwood was the pawn he was almost afraid to move.

Sweat formed on his face. He had never felt so close to riches; nor, for several years, so close to being broke. He remembered his grimy past, remembered the thousand dwindling bankrolls. Broke—in a trade where you had to look sharp and prosperous; where you skipped meals to buy halfsoles, did your own tailor-work, cared for your hands like a surgeon. And for these sacrifices you were entitled to inhabit a world of murky gambling-rooms and anticipate the day when some drunken loser would wait in an alley to put a bullet in your back.

Almost in panic, he bounced up and went to the wall-map on which his mine-holdings were pin-pointed. Hands in pockets, he stood studying it. There were traces of gold in all the silver ore in this country, and a few exhausted goldmines. With Croft's process it would be profitable to work all the old tailings and mine-dumps, reopen some of the burned-out stopes they'd abandoned years ago. Of course all those properties were owned by someone; he'd have to track them down, lease them the way Freeman had leased half-a-county of tailings from him.

But dammit, he realized, the edge beginning to chip off his exultation, Freeman held a two-year lease on most of his own properties! How could he buy them back without making Freeman suspicious? Or what if Jessie went to Freeman for money to buy the process? Even after he got the money to pay Croft, he had to get a world of properties, fast. For Jessie might publish the news herself, just for spite.

Haines blew out the lamp and hurried to the bank on the windswept corner. The half-shades were drawn, but in the rear he saw a light burning inside Brickwood's velour domain. He rapped, and could have sworn the office door budged open a crack, and someone looked out. But though he continued knocking, no one showed up.

Haines strode down to the Two Nation Saloon to look for the banker. Time was pressing against his throat like a knife. Since it was supper-time, it was surprising to find a fair crowd at the saloon, most of them gathered in small, earnest groups around the tables. As he passed down the bar, he sensed their sudden watchfulness and a monitor in his brain raised a finger. Fletcher Henry came up with his bottle of whisky.

"Carl Brickwood been around?" Haines asked him.

"Not since noon. Where you been, Tom? Kinda dropped out of sight."

"What do you want me to do—stand here with my foot on the rail all day?"

Fletch raised his skinny shoulders. "Johnny Keeley was looking for you, that's all."

"Keeley! He was in the cooler this morning."

"That was before Marshal Wilks found out the sheriff wouldn't be here for another four days. Got a telegram. Wilks was afraid to hold him that long."

Haines summoned a smile. "How's Johnny taking his freedom? Like a gentleman?"

Henry gave his pop-eyed grin. "He's up in his room. Packing for a trip, I expect. Maybe a trip would do him good."

"A trip would do Freeman good," Haines said shortly. "That boy's got a problem." He drank his whisky, shook his head when Fletch Henry started to refill the glass. But all at once he grew conscious of the silence of the room. He thought, *Wait a minute—what's going on?* The saloonkeeper made a swipe with the bar-towel as he turned to walk back to the balcony stairs.

"Say, Tom—" he said. "Did Freeman do any good on them old mill-tailings of yours? I mean, did you have any way of knowing what he was making?"

The tough gray muscle behind Haines's eyes convulsed with surprise and anger. What went on? Had Jessie spilled it already? Had Keeley been reading his mail? He turned back slowly and said,

"He made day-wages. If he made more, he never reported it."

"Think there was much gold in that stuff?"

"How could there be? It was worked for both gold and silver the first time around. What's the matter—is pouring whisky getting too hard for you?"

"Just wondering."

"Wondering what?" Haines persisted.

Henry shrugged. Some poker-chips clattered somewhere and a man cleared his throat. "Oh—just wondering how he made out."

"Well, let me know if you find out he was making a killing. He was supposed to pay me a percentage of all he refined."

"I'll do that!" Henry went away chuckling.

You little wolf! though Haines viciously. *What the hell's up now?* He headed up the stairs for Keeley's room.

Crouched on his cot behind the door, Johnny Keeley was rasping with a triangular file on a small flat piece of metal. He stared at Haines with savage, bloodshot eyes in a battered face. Haines saw a new Colt revolver, dismantled, lying on the blankets. Keeley was filing off the sear—first requirement of the snap-shot artist. Dressed in trousers and socks, the gunman exhibited a shallow chest and bony shoulders, with some discolorations on his chest as though it, as well as his face, had taken punishment from the beating Shep Freeman had given him.

Haines said drily, "You look mighty professional, John. A lot more professional than you must have looked in that hopper-car."

Keeley lunged to his feet and kicked the door shut. Then he caught Haines by surprise by suddenly thrusting him against the wall with his forearm across his windpipe.

"You want the first shot I make out of that Colt? Is that what you're sayin'?"

"Oh, you could drop me—if everything was right. That's the trouble with you, boy—too many things throw you off-balance."

The pressure of Keeley's arm increased. Haines felt a hand dip under his coat, slyly, and snatch the small house-gun from its spring holster under his arm. The barrel of the gun sank deep into Haines's gut.

"Not everything—" grinned Keeley. "Just fellers dropping out of the sky on top of me. Or clipping me behind the ear while you watch. That's the only kind of stuff bothers me."

I've got a whole deck full of stuff like that, Haines thought. And was glad Keeley had done this, since it smoothed the burrs off a big, final decision he had been unwilling to handle.

"When you get done, I want to talk to you," he said huskily, choked by Keeley's forearm. Presently the gunman lowered his arm, threw the gun on the bed, and stepped back.

"Talk nice, then," he suggested. "Don't talk funny like you do sometimes. Johnny's gettin' tired of it. I set up there waitin' for you to go my bail, and gettin' sick of your fancy talk with nothin' behind it."

Haines massaged his throat. "You must have been giving them some fancy talk downstairs, yourself. Fletch Henry was curious about where I was today. And how much gold Freeman was taking out of those tailings."

A sheepish smile touched Keeley's mouth. "Don't blame me. Everybody wanted to know how-come me to be riding in a hopper-car, and I told them you wanted some tailings samples. Reckon when nobody could find you today, they got curious."

"How much help did you give them in figuring it out?"

"That's all. What I told you." Keeley sat on the cot and picked up the file, avoiding his eyes.

"That was enough! The assayer would pass it around that I'd had the tailings assayed; the stable would mention I'd rented a wagon this morning. That was plenty!"

Panic fluttered up in him again like a moth. Keeley's file

whispered back and forth on the brittle steel, but he did not explain. Haines saw that revenge obsessed him completely. That was all right, too. But the shot needed to be fired so that somebody besides Keeley would profit. It was not yet clear to him how it might be done. But there was no question but that Johnny Keeley was going to start earning his salary.

"You know you're going to be in trouble when Freeman gives his story to the sheriff, don't you?" Haines asked.

Keeley's swollen eye tilted rakishly. "He ain't going to testify. He's all done testifying."

"Suit yourself. Hang for whichever murder you want, or both. If it was me, I wouldn't hang at all. And I'd square things with Freeman without going to all the trouble you are."

The file chattered on. "It ain't no trouble."

"No. The trouble will come later. If you're seen, then you're a dead one when they catch you. If you aren't, you've got to establish an alibi."

A flicker of irritation passed over Keeley's face. "Maybe I'll travel."

"Where? To South America? Wake up!" Haines said barshly. "Guns are pretty, but an accident will beat one every time. And mines are murder for accidents."

At last Keeley lay over on one elbow and dropped the file. "What kinda accident did you have in mind?"

Haines felt a wash of relief. "Come over to the office in the morning," he winked. "We've got to go up to Hornitos on Saturday with the payroll. We'll figure out how much everybody's got coming tomorrow."

"I can tell you how much Freeman's got coming without using a pencil," Keeley told him.

20

ACTING ON SHEP'S INSTRUCTIONS, Grady Galloway shot the first series of holes at the mine while Shep was in Travertine waiting for Johnny Keeley. The next day, the powder-smoke and dust having cleared, the mucking-out was done. Shep went into the tunnel to inspect the results of the blast. It had deepened a hole which Haines's engineers had begun in the foot-wall halfway down the main tunnel. It was now a shallow pit, a winze, funneling down fifteen feet below floor-level. A catwalk had been rigged along the sidewall, and Shep passed over the winze flashing a lamp at the exposed rock below him. Everywhere it looked good. He had a tingle of prosperous gooseflesh.

It might be worthwhile to take a deep shaft down from the bottom of the hole and drive a tunnel in to intersect it much deeper. In this way the winze could be deepened and enlarged and all the loosened rock would fall down the shaft and be removed easily through the lower tunnel.

Shep crossed the excavation and went on to the end of the tunnel, where a shaft ascended to an upper test-tunnel. Flashing his carbide mine-lamp, he saw the rich colors of the ore, and he took a long, pleased breath. How could you lose in a mine like this? All you needed to decide was the cheapest way to hollow out the hill.

When he went back he saw Bill Croft climbing gingerly from an ore-wagon, his peg-leg groping for the ground. Grady Galloway came up the little rail-line from the ore-bin at the edge of the bench, and he and Croft walked to where Shep was hanging his lamp beside the timbered entrance. Croft grinned a greeting, and Shep noiced his indrawn upper lip.

"What happened to the uppers, Bill?" he asked.

"My old lady needed 'em for choppin' steak today. Like my leg, they're detachable. How's she look?" he asked, nodding at the mine.

"She looks like this." Shep squatted on the ground and drew a slanting line representing the slope of the hill. Then he drew a horizontal line in from the first to represent the tunnel. Above it he drew a parallel line—the tunnel whose entrance was farther up the hill. He connected the two by a vertical shaft, and sketched in, below the main tunnel, the pit he had just inspected.

"The ore's as rich one place as another," he said. "The winze might be the best bet, though. If we make a funnel out of it, we can glory-hole the ore out below. What do you think?"

Croft shook his head. "Take 'er up. Clean out the attic before you tackle the basement. The deeper you go, the higher your costs."

"Not at this depth. And if we glory-hole, we can be working the upper tunnel at the same time, can't we?"

Croft flushed and stood up. "Take 'er up! Take 'er down. Take 'er crosswise! I thought you wanted my opinion. If you've already got your mind made up, why ask me?"

Both men stared at him. "Teeth aren't all you lost, Bill," Shep told him. "Look around for your temper when you go back. There're more sharp corners to you than a box of dice."

"If I'm in your way," Croft huffed, "I'll go back right now. Excuse me."

Shep and Galloway laughed, and Croft's lips tightened. Just then the sentry at the road shouted. Until Haines proved he was ready to work, Shep had decided to maintain a guard around the clock. A big man in gray work-clothes stood with the sentry, a roll of plans under his arm.

"By George, it's Dennis!" said Galloway.

Shep signaled Dennis inside. They waited by the mine-entrance while the superintendent crossed the ground, glancing critically at everything that was being done. "Walks like he owned the place," growled Galloway. Once the superintendent stopped to glare up at a partially-finished gallows-frame, shook his head and came on. Reaching them, he removed his hat and dropped it on the ground; put out his chin and inspected them one by one. At last he handed Shep the roll of plans.

"Haines says we go back to work. Here's the engineers' idea of how we do it."

Shep accepted the plans and offered his hand. Dennis said, "Make a fist of that and offer it to me. Then maybe we can make a deal."

Shep saw the resentment in his eyes. Still, he must have wrestled with his pride all night before he could even force himself to report for work. Shep unrolled the plans and Galloway helped pin them to the ground with stones. Plan and section, they were a detailed diagram of what Shep had drawn on the ground. But the excavation he had been arguing with Croft was shown, in shading, as an enormous gloryhole tapped far below by a tunnel for the removal of ore.

"How do we go about it?" he asked Dennis.

"We should start the tunnel today. At the same time we'll be making the big shots in the winze—haul the rock out the main tunnel until we finish the one below."

"Big shots?" Croft asked suspiciously. "How big?"

"Ask the geologists. I'm the muscles and they're the brains."

"But you'll use six-foot drills to finish?"

His jaw setting, Dennis retorted: "Is it you I'm doin' business with now, you old mine-rat?"

"No, but it's a good question," Shep told him.

Dennis sounded as though he had memorized it. "We drill

until the hole's six feet deep. Then we use a drill-and-bar to deepen it to eight feet.''

''Eight-foot holes, eh?'' Croft said, narrow-eyed. ''How many of them at a shot?''

Dennis cleared his throat. ''Twelve.''

''Twelve!'' said Galloway. ''Do any of you men mind loud noises?''

''The hell with the noise,'' snapped Dennis. ''It's only a few more holes than regular.''

''And each one two feet deeper,'' reminded Croft. ''Freeman, I tell you he'll blow the top off this hill! It'll be days before you can work the mine again, and then you'll be dealin' with widow-making cracks from there on in.''

Dennis crossed his arms, turned his back and gazed at a mule-team pulling a scraper, but said nothing. ''I've seen it done before,'' Shep recalled. ''There was no trouble.''

''Open-pit, maybe.'' Now Bill Croft straightened and looked Shep in the eye. ''I've got a personal interest in this mine, my boy, because I staked my reputation on it. But that was assuming it was worked by men in their right minds. I withdraw my interest in it, now. I tell you that if you shoot them holes as Dennis wants, your Sweet Betsy will be blowed clean back to Pike County. That's my last word to you.''

Dennis's big shoulders stirred as he shifted his weight to his other foot. Galloway, feeling bound to back up Croft, muttered:

''Might be he's right, Freeman.''

Shep frowned into the tunnel and tucked in his shirt-tail. ''Might be. But right or wrong, I'll show good faith this time by going along with Haines's geologists. If she caves in— then I've learned my lesson.''

Bill Croft walked off a few paces, turned back and shouted with a red face: ''You'll learn it all right! But you'll be a poor man like me when you do.''

Charlie Dennis smiled at him now with iron malice. ''What's wrong down there in the guts of this hill, Croft? You were so hot for it before. You had Haines believing his ore would be labeled, *In God We Trust*. Now you want to mine up, instead of down! What's a-matter here? Are we heading for an underground river that'll wash us out like it done Tombstone?''

The Cornishman turned his back and hobbled off toward the wagon-road. Uneasiness touched Shep like a cold puff of mine-damp. These Cousin Jacks with their moods and hunches, nursing them like sickly children until the things invaded their minds. What could you ask of a mine but that its ore ran wide and deep and rich? Yet Croft undeniably harbored a fear that the mine suffered from some mysterious sickness. He turned and gazed into the tunnel, and then Dennis slapped his hands together and said loudly:

''Well, boys, let's be filling our pockets with silver, hey? Bring me your huskiest drillers, Galloway. Mr. Haines will be up day after tomorrow with the payroll, and he wants to watch that first shot himself, before we go on with the plan.''

The lunch triangle clanged. As Shep started for the washtrough, Dennis added: ''By the way, Doctor. One of your patients, Johnny Keeley, was discharged as cured by Marshal Wilks yesterday. It seems like the sheriff won't be here for the better part of a week, and the marshal was afraid Johnny'd get restless. Any word for the boy, in case he comes askin' for you?''

''Yes: Take off,'' Shep snapped. ''You've done a lot of bragging about how good a mine superintendent you are, Dennis. Now let's see you perform.''

''You'll see me,'' Dennis promised.

After the noon meal, Shep took a sledge-hammer and a two-and-a-half-inch drill and stopped at the mine-entrance for a lamp. He added a little water, struck the flint and fixed the hissing lamp to his cap. Dennis came out of the tunnel, blinking in the sunlight. Seeing him, he began to laugh.

''Ah, he's one of the democratic owners!'' he said. ''No better than any of your men, eh?''

''But just as good.'' Shep put the sledge over his shoulder. His temper was brittle, and he required none of Dennis's heavyfooted joshing just now.

"Just as good, is it?—You, there!" Dennis bawled at a man across the bench. "Bring me a sledge. —So you were a hardrock man before you were an owner, were you? I'll bet I doublejack you to your knees."

"For how much?"

"I'm a poor man, Doctor. Say a free whack at the chin of the loser?"

In his face brimmed the same old resentment and jealousy gone sour and biting as vinegar. All his life he had been proving his worth with his fists. Now he had lost once, and the failure remained in him like a thorn, poisoning and irritating his mind. If he lost another contest, the splintered ends of his ego would probably cut Dennis to pieces. But it was Dennis's own problem if he had to pick fights and stake everything on them.

"The loser to keep his eyes open while the fist travels," Shep amended Dennis's wager. "Get yourself a helper. You've got yourself a bet."

21

THE FLOOR OF THE EXCAVATION made a rough arena for the four men taking part in the contest. Blasted about fifteen feet below the level of the tunnel, the excavation was long and narrow, its ends pitching steeply up to the tunnel-floor and faced with broken rock. At either end a number of drills had been placed, the longest of them six feet long. Buckets of water were in readiness to settle the dust. Above the winze, miners crowded the tunnel and catwalk to watch the contest.

Dennis had stripped off his shirt. The deep torso with its diamond of black hair on the chest had the stark whiteness of quartz. He pulled his belt up tight, flexed his arms, and called to Shep, who was thumping the handle of his sledge-hammer against the floor:

"Save your strength, Doctor. Is that the end you pick?"

"Hell, no!" Grady Galloway retorted. Shep had picked him for his helper. "It's the end you didn't camp on. Your spot is rotten with tufa. We'll toss a coin."

They tossed, and Dennis won. "I'll work this end," he said.

Galloway grumbled as he looked for a spot in the porphyry to set the star-drill. He selected a place about a foot from the slanting end-wall and set the drill against it. "How's this?"

Shep looked at it. It was very dense stone, and from the look of the recently blasted ore lying about, it would be solid. He laid his hammer over his shoulder and called to Dennis that the was ready. He kicked the loose rock away while a miner up above counted for the start.

"On your marks!... get set..."

The two hammers rang against the splayed drill-ends. Shep's bounced back as though it had struck an anvil. A small scatter of rock-chips was loosened. He swung again as Galloway turned the drill. Chips flew and rock-dust drifted. The drill with its sharp-edged plus-sign still had not made itself a decent dimple. On the next swing, Shep blasted the point a quarter-inch into the gray stone. And he knew there was no charity at all in his end of the excavation.

After a while Charlie Dennis panted, "Four-foot drill!" Shep heard his helper drop the two-foot drill, slop some water into the hole, and ram home the four-foot bar. His own drill was about a foot deep, now. Dennis was eight or ten inches ahead of him already. The sweat ran from him freely but he was not tired. He heard Dennis cough.

Dennis finished the second drill in fine time, driving steadily, and he was not working hard. The broad back and shoulders worked rhythmically. Shep had to ask for fresh drills several times before he changed to the four-foot drill. Each time, water was quickly poured into the hole. The shock of the sledge against that tough porphyry was making his joints ache. It brought back the day he graduated from mucker to miner, and went home so tired from punishing those almost unused muscles that he could not sleep for the aches in him—like his father, who had hammered at the rock so long his whole body ached, crying out against dampness, and fatigue that was a chronic disease. It made him feel faintly guilty under the eyes of his miners, now, that he should be playing a game of mining, like a game of horseshoes, while they were chained to the trade. But unless he got complete cooperation out of Dennis, and threw some ringers in his game with Haines, he would be back in those chains himself....

Three feet into the hole, he felt a sudden crumbling of the rock. Gray with the stone-mud which splattered back from the drill, Galloway glanced up at him. The drill had penetrated an inch in a single stroke. Galloway hastily revolved the drill and again Shep rolled the sledge home. The drill bit in three inches, and Galloway grinned and made a big show of turning the drill.

"You're in a fissure!" he whispered. "Make it look hard. Let him wear himself out."

But it was difficult to make it look hard. The drill seemed to have penetrated a wall. Soon Galloway bawled: "Six-foot drill!" and there was some chatter from the miners as the Irishman rammed the final drill into the hole, for Dennis had barely started on his own last two feet. Dennis, his mine-cough tearing at him, was laboring. He was in harder rock than before. But at each of Shep's light swings the drill jumped from the hammer deeper into the rock.

It was strange, and he did not understand it. He had hit a pocket, he knew that for certain. A pocket like a volcanic blowhole, but it was not volcanic country.

"Will you get me a decent drill, damn it?" he heard Dennis's angry gasp. Metal rasped and clinked while drills were changed. Shep punched steadily and the hole devoured the drill. Dennis's sledging increased in tempo. Once Shep glanced around and saw the white wedge of his back glistening with sweat. Above him were the tense faces of the miners, their satisfaction tucked into the lines of their mouths.

He swung once more and the drill was gone.

Galloway stared at the hole, then up at Shep. Shep felt for the edges of the drill-head, caught a hold and drew it out. The miners began whooping. Dennis turned to see what had happened. Shep dropped his sledge and rubbed his hands together.

"That's it," he said.

Dennis tramped over to stare at the eye in the stone. He shoved a six-foot drill into it, pulled it out and dropped it. His face and torso were as wet as though he had swum a river. He was gray and whipped, and gasping as he breathed. Planting his fists on his hips, he panted:

"Can you find my chin, or do you want an X on it?"

Shep mopped his face with his shirt. "Take care of it for me. I'll claim my prize when I want it."

"*"Take it now!"* roared the superintendent.

The craggy face was red, his mouth quivered. Shep hit him fast, clean but not hard; yet with no fat in the punch, so that Dennis floundered back and sat down. He shook his head and spat between his spread legs. Then in a sudden angry scramble he came to his feet and lunged at Shep with his fist cocked. Shep stood there. Dennis halted, passed his palm across his face and said:

"Excuse it. It's in the nature to fight back, you know."

"I'll excuse nature every time. I hope you'll do the same."

Galloway said later, "You should have strung him out longer—let him dig his grave with that sledge."

"That's what I was afraid of his doing. What did I drill into?"

"Just a pint-sized blow-hole or fissure. It don't happen often, but that's the time it happened nicely."

The drilling continued the rest of that day and the next, and the twelve holes Tom Haines's engineers wanted were completed by sundown. Powder was rolled in newspapers and inserted into the holes, packed hard with wooden dowels, and fuses and tamping were rammed in. In the morning Haines would be up with the payroll and personally supervise the blasting. Friday night, when Shep rode back to Hornitos on an ore-wagon, he found Fletch Henry in the saloon where he was batching, measuring the walls with the assistance of a carpenter. In one corner was Shep's cot, separated from the ancient rubble by a low barricade of crates. "What's the idea?" he asked.

Henry set his derby askew and rolled up his tape. "I've leased this place from Tom Haines," he said briskly. "The plans he's got for the mine, Hornitos'll be a boom-town again. His men will be quartered here. There'll be more prospectors around these hills than miners, especially after the election."

"I suppose you want me to move."

"Oh, no hurry!" said Henry open-handedly. "Take a week to find something else. Oh, say—Haines asked me to tell you he'd pay the men right here. Then you'll all go up to the mine as planned."

Shep got unaccountably restless that evening, and finally walked up to the Crofts' and asked to see Drusilla. Mrs. Croft said Dru was washing her hair. She was going to Travertine tomorrow and must be in bed early. He drifted back, trying to picture the ghost-town as a boom-town again. It was hard, though, with coyotes yipping on a near ridge and a fox loping soundlessly across the road as he returned to the saloon. Fletcher Henry and his man had departed and left the door open. He stood beside it for a few moments, not sure whether it was the quiet mountain night he was reluctant to leave, or the ruined saloon he disliked to enter.

That afternoon Tom Haines cleaned up some details.

At the bank, he visited Carl Brickwood in his velour-bound domain. Brickwood sat behind his desk looking weary and driven. The skin beneath his eyes was puckered. Haines handed him a deposit slip he had made out previously.

"For your convenience, Carl," he said, "I've dated it today. Regarding that Sweet Betsy stock you're buying."

Brickwood frowned at the deposit slip, which stated that on this day ten thousand dollars was to be placed in the mine account. "By sheer coincidence," he said sourly, "I was just mulling this over myself! I don't see how I can do it."

"Maybe you can figure it out in Yuma, then."

"If I do make it," Brickwood declared stonily, "I'll be

putting myself in jeopardy in another direction—eating into my legal reserves.''

''If it will make it any easier, I'll tell you something: Freeman and I are going to be working together after all. So you can open your mill. And you'll be pulling dividends on your mine-stock at the same time.''

''That's—that's good news, Tom!.. Brickwood brightened. ''But you said it would have to be a hundred percent of the mine or you couldn't survive. So how can he stay in the game?''

Haines smiled. ''Give me a little time, Carl. The mills of the gods grind slow. I'll want the cash before three.''

Brickwood sighed. ''You might as well take it with you. What's it to be used for?''

''Read the annual report,'' Haines winked.

On the walk he lingered a moment. He was breathless, with a quivering in his knees. From this instant, everything he did and said must be directed toward one final act, though it must seem undirected and casual.

Yet there was absolutely no time to dally. Keeley's and the assayer's chatter had generated a secret but nonetheless frantic market in leases on old mines. Five men had dropped in at the office today and casually asked whether he had any tailings or marginal mines he cared to lease...oh, just a crazy notion there might be a few grains of gold and silver left in them, they would hastily assure him. Crazy like a fox! All over town, leases were being bought and sold under the counter, while men waited to learn whether a new gold-recovery process was about to be announced.

Haines needed to talk to Keeley, now, but he hesitated to seek him openly, because tomorrow when everyone was mulling over the accident in the mine someone might say, ''That's funny—I remember Tom Haines came for Johnny about four o'clock—and just after dark Johnny left town...''

Now, wait, he told himself reasonably. *He works for you, doesn't he? He's your paymaster, and tomorrow's payday.*

You have things to talk over with him. Why not?

He went to the Two Nations. Fletch was not behind the bar. A barkeeper told him, "He went up to Hornitos this morning. He's fixing to open up one of the old bars, there."

"Well, is Keeley here?"

The barkeeper sent for Keeley, who came down the stairs looking sleepy, pulling his sleeves up and adjusting pale-blue sleeve-garters. He yawned while a drink was poured for him.

"What are you doing—going into your long winter nap?" Haines asked him.

"There was a big game last night." Keeley gingerly let the liquor sting his tongue. "Say—tomorrow's payday, ain't it? There ought to be a lot of action here tomorrow night. I reckon you want me to go up and pay off the miners, eh?"

Loud enough for people to hear, Haines said: "Not this time. Not until you and Freeman get over your peeve. That's what I wanted to see you about. Just forget it for a couple of weeks. No use antagonizing him."

"Suit yourself," Keeley said. Then Haines tilted his head slightly toward the street door, and Keeley closed one eyed and nodded.

Ten minutes after Haines returned to his office, Keeley came in the back way. Haines was ready for him. He laid a sheet of paper on the table and started to draw a diagram on it. "Memorize this," he said, "because I'm going to burn it up when we're finished." He was not really frightened. There was no reason to be frightened. But he could not breathe very deeply and his hands were trembling: buck fever.

"The top line is the upper tunnel," he said. He made his voice deep and calm. "Do you know where it is?"

Keeley's eyes were sober and intent. "I was right near it when—"

Haines smiled at the slip. "*...when I shot Willy Matteson,*" the statement would have been finished. "Just so you know where it is," he said. "Now. The entrance to it is about two hundred feet up the slope from the bench, and pretty well screened with mesquite. At the end of the tunnel a shaft drops to the main tunnel. There's a fixed ladder. When you step off it, you'll be standing at the end of the main tunnel, and if you walk about a hundred feet you'll come to the winze they've been blasting.... Still with me?'' he asked.

''Prob'ly ahead of you. They've drilled some new holes in the winze and they're waiting for you before they set them off, right?''

''Right. Where do you come in it?''

''You tell me.''

''I will, if I get a chance. Freeman and I and a couple of others will go in and look things over. The others will go out in a few minutes, and I'll follow them. Freeman will be delayed. He'll stay in there quite a while, working at whatever it is that's holding us up. Deepening a hole, maybe. You'll see me come out, and that's your signal to go down and light the match. It'll be a five-minute fuse. You'll have time to kill.''

Keeley looked up from the diagram, silently frowning. The wide, sharp cheekbones enhanced the hollowness of his face. He waited.

''When I come out,'' Haines continued, ''I'll tell the others Freeman is going to be out in a minute. He doesn't come out, and finally I tell them I'm going in and see whether he's sprained his ankle or something. That's were the timing is important, Johnny. Five minutes after we leave the tunnel, you've got to strike the match.''

''Five minutes,'' Keeley nodded.

''And you've got five minutes more to get back and wait in the adit of the upper tunnel for the blast. After the excitement begins, you can take off. And if I were you, I'd keep riding.''

Keeley's eyes lidded sardonically. ''Pretty big favor I'm doing you, Thomas.''

''Oh, no. You're doing it for both of us. Because his testimony about Matteson might weave a hangrope for you.''

He began tearing the map into strips; cross-tore the strips, dropped them into the heat-stove and burned them. They made a tiny fire in the bottom of it. He closed the iron door and looked at Keeley.

"And there'll be five thousand dollars in the mail for you in a few months. Just send me your address."

"Now you're talking my language," Keeley smiled. He walked to the alley door. "I'll go up tonight."

22

IN THE MORNING THE ghost-town of Hornitos tingled with an
air of things doing, and Dru caught some of its excitement as
she walked to the station. Miners roamed the old, worm-
eaten boardwalks; a few horses were staked in the vacant lots
and a dray was being unloaded at the stonefront Cloverleaf
Bar. None of the miners was drunk yet, and they all behaved
politely and tipped their hats to a young lady obviously
dressed for Travertine. She assumed they had not been paid,
or else there was nowhere to buy liquor.

In her handbag she carried the gold for Uncle Virgil. In her
mind she rehearsed what she must do. They had concluded
that it would be wise to ask for a two- or three-week supply of
leaching brine, on the ground that Hornitos was becoming so
active that they might have to move to another area for greater
secrecy. Lately there had been men roaming the hills with the
unrealistic ardor of prospectors in their eyes. Dru, however,
was not so unrealistic as to hope that Uncle Virgil would
agree to the request.

She heard a bell-clanging—the payroll train was arriving. She reached the weed-grown depot as it pulled in—
four flat-cars of supplies, and a coach. Jake Lund and Tom
Haines dismounted. Haines was carrying a brown valise
closed with a little brass padlock. He saw Dru and

smilingly raised his hat.

"Tell your father to put the blessing of the little people on us," he said. "We're starting in earnest today."

Despite his smile, he seemed to regard her with keen, humorless interest. He looked weary, somewhat pallid, like a man just off a spree.

"You'll have to tell him yourself," she said. "I'm taking the train back. Unless it's waiting for you?"

"No, it'll leave those flats on the siding and go back for some more. How's the work at Mill Number Three?"

"All right," she shrugged.

Haines hit Lund with his elbow. "All right! Bet she's got more in the bank than we have, eh, Jake?"

She did not answer, but saw an expression in his eyes of sly amusement. It made her uneasy.

In Travertine, it was so hot that she rented a turnout. The meatless old gray took nearly an hour to deliver her to her uncle's adobe hut. Virgil came to the mosquito-bar door and gave her a long, blank stare.

"I—I have the gold, uncle," she said at last.

Surprised, he accepted the paper-wrapped slug of gold. "Well, well! Come in." He weighed it on his troy scale and set it aside. He asked after everyone's health, and with growing nervousness she said everybody was fine.

"Ain't that nice?" he said. There was a slant of lunacy in his grin.

"How are you going to divide the gold?" she asked finally.

"Want to show you some nice spurs I bought for my fightin' cocks," he said. He took a match-box from a shelf above the stove, set Chucho, his bantam rooster, on the table and took the spurs from the box. They had been made out of thin metal, were red on one side and shinily tinned on the other. He fixed them to the rooster's legs.

"Of course I wouldn't know one spur from another," Dru said uninterestedly.

"Oh, you ought to know these spurs, niece," he scoffed.

"Why?"

His face distorted. "Because a Mex made them out of the tin can your pellets were in! He found it in the train! He told me he threw the pellets in the wash, and later I heard three goats died. Oh, your uncle ain't very acute, Drusilla, but he could put *them* pieces together! Where'd you get this gold?"

"Dad's teeth," she said numbly.

The room shrilled with his laughter. "His teeth! Oh, my Lord! He's wasted more money on those teeth than most men do on liquor."

She went to the door. "Uncle, it was my fault, not his. The train stopped fast and threw all my things on the floor. Somehow I missed the tobacco can. If you'll trust us once more . . ."

"Too late." Croft shrugged. "I'm selling it."

She remembered his threat to sell. "Not to Tom Haines?" she asked.

"Or his sister."

"Does Jessie have any money?"

Croft winked. "She's got a rich sweetheart. Her and her brother are jockeyin' around for the process. After I demonstrated it the other day, she came back and told me she thought she could raise twenty thousand cash if I'd give her a few days. Her friend had more or less promised it to her."

The cheap little schemer! thought Dru. *Dragging Shep into a thing like this! He'll lose anything he salvages out of the mine, and get nothing for it. . . . Or is that really what bothers me? If I don't want him myself, why should I care that another woman does—for love, money, or what?*

"You won't need the gold, then," she said sharply, and went back for it. She reached it before he did, and when he laid a hand on her wrist she faced him with a sudden black fury in her eyes. "You dirty old miser!" she said. "Take you hand away."

His hand dropped, and in his astonishment he let her walk out undisciplined.

After a table had been set up in the doorway of the Cloverleaf Saloon, Jake Lund sat down with the satchel of money and the time-sheets, and the waiting miners in the street began to line up.

"Where's our official paymaster?" Shep asked Haines. "I hear he's out again."

"Wilks couldn't hold him."

"And hell won't have him, if he comes up here. You may call him a paymaster, but I call him a target." He stared at Haines, but Haines's smile told him nothing. "All right, let's go," Shep said. "Dennis and Galloway are waiting for us."

"How do you travel—shank's mares?"

"There's a wagon in back."

Only a dozen men were at the mine when they arrived, most of them working on the ore-chute. Seated on the ground near the main tunnel, Dennis was smoking a pipe. He got up and dusted the seat of his pants as they turned the wagon over to a teamster.

"How's she look, Charlie?" Haines asked enthusiastically.

The Irishman gazed down the strap-iron railway at the lumbering, overalled figure of Grady Galloway, tramping up from the ore-chute. "Like the plan you gave me," he said.

While Dennis lighted lamps, Haines stripped off his coat and gazed up the slope. The mesquite was dense, except where it had been hacked away. "Have you started any work in Number Two tunnel?"

"Not yet. We've had worries enough down here."

Haines took the mine-cap Dennis handed him. In his white shirt and dark trousers he looked square-shouldered and vigorous. But his face, Shep thought, appeared strained as he looked at his pocket-watch, returned it to his pocket, and again scrutinized the slope.

"What time is it?" Shep asked with a grin.

Haines blinked, then laughed. "I didn't look. I was thinking about something Charlie said the other day. 'You'll blow the lid off with all that powder!' I claim we won't—but I must have my doubts." He looked at the watch. "One fifteen." Still chuckling, he lighted a rum-soaked cigar.

The four men tramped along the narrow rails into the tunnel which ran straight back for some distance before making a gentle swing to the left. At the deep, jagged excavation where the charges had been set, Dennis clambered down the rocks and set his boot beside a fuse trailing from a little mound of clay. He looked up with a sour smile, which vanished in a swift scowl.

"No smoking, dammit!" he snapped.

Haines gazed blankly at his cigar. "I should know better than that," he said mildly. He broke off the glowing tip on a rock and discarded the cigar.

"I was going to say that I drilled this hole myself," Dennis continued; then, walking to the other end of the winze: "And Mr. Freeman drilled this one—in half the time it took me. He's a rare one, Mr. Haines. A miner, a fighter, and a good judge of knockout drops."

"Shut up, Charlie," Haines sighed. "Am I going to have to find a new super after all?"

"You are. I find I can't work here. I can't tell you why, exactly, but part of it is my own crusty nature. So I'll draw my time after today and maybe Galloway will suit you better."

"The black moods of the Irish," Galloway mourned. "Shut up like the gentleman says, and tell us what's going to happen."

Shep felt sorry for Dennis, a tough, honest man whose code had failed him because it was too rigid. It did not include personal failure, nor doing things someone else's way when you thought it was wrong.

"I mean it," Dennis said quietly. "But for the present, I see it this way: there's little risk the way we've placed the conduit holes. Most of the force will go down as it should. But of course we'll be a week muckin' out."

Shep watched Haines climb down and inspect the angles of the holes, then gaze up at the dim hanging-wall and scratch his ear. "I don't know. I think a couple of stulls would cancel out any danger there might be."

"How's that?" Dennis asked.

Haines stretched out his arms. "Wedge them crosswise just below the level of the tunnel."

Dennis cleared his throat. "I don't believe I've seen it done just that way before."

"Then I judge it should never be done?" countered Haines.

Dennis's face set. "Shall I get the timbers?"

"On the double. You and Galloway can probably carry them alone. If not, pick up some carpenters to help you, or put them on a car. Shep," he joked, "you don't mean you really drilled a hole all by yourself?"

"I wish I could say it was the first."

Haines climbed back up to the tunnel. Dennis and Galloway tramped into the darkness. Haines stood beside Shep, panting a little as he frowned into the now dark excavation, where damp glints of lamplight were thrown back from the stones. "It may be awkward to rig up," he said. He was holding a short wooden tamper as a pointer. "We could wedge one end of the stull in that little hollow, there. The other—"

When he did not finish, Shep glanced at him. He saw Haines features distort with a kind of wildness as the wooden bar thudded against his head. It was not a solid blow, but it stunned him, and he fell to his knees. He groped with one hand for support. Haines struck again, but he was falling sidewise and the club struck his forehead. He went rolling and sprawling down the slope into the excavation. His mine-lamp fell off and went out; when he stopped rolling he was in absolute blackness. He knew Haines would be after him in a moment, but was unable to move or even care very much.

Haines started to follow him, but halted to pick up Freeman's lamp and flash it on him. He was not moving. Let well enough alone, he thought, suddenly wanting to get out of this tunnel. He had never been aware of the weight of all the rock above him in a mine before, but now it seemed to be crushing him. He scrambled back to the tunnel and hurried along the tracks toward the adit.

When he saw the sunlight ahead, he wanted to run to it. Instead, he halted, leaned against the side-wall and breathed deeply for a few moments, until he was able to walk calmly into the daylight. He saw Dennis and Galloway plodding toward the mine with a short, heavy timber linking their shoulders like a bridge. Already! He turned, with a grip of panic, to stare up the hill at they upper tunnel. There was a stir of movement, then nothing at all, and he knew Keeley was hurrying down the tunnel.

He stopped Dennis, who was leading. "Put it down," he sighed. "I was afriad you'd bring a matchstick like that. I thought I could catch you in time. Isn't there an eight-by-eight around?"

"Yes, sir," Dennis said with the grim politeness of a trooper who, with his discharge coming up, doesn't want to jeopardize his freedom.

"Let's see what's in the pile. You didn't get a sledge, either."

Johnny Keeley wished he had brought a mine-lamp instead of a candle. But he was traveling light—everything he owned rolled behind his saddle. He had left his horse across the ridge. As he was climbing down the ladder to the main tunnel, the draft extinguished his candle and he had to slow down and grope. Reaching the tunnel, he relighted his candle and started off. About a hundred feet, Haines had said. He hurried along, making a reflector of one hand to protect the candle. Again it blew out, and he drew from his pocket a single match, then in alarm dug through his pockets for more. There were no more. He sucked a breath in through his teeth. Hell, if the candle went out again—

Blindly he started off with the candle unlighted. But soon he got to worrying about falling into the pit, and he stopped and struck the match.

He started. He was standing about five feet from the edge of the winze! Hurriedly he transferred the flame to the black wick of the candle. He could scarcely make out the shape of the excavation. At the bottom he peered around owlishly for

Freeman's body, saw him lying about fifteen feet away and studied him a moment. There was blood on his head. He was not moving.

He walked over to retrieve Freeman's lamp, lying up the slope a couple of yards, struck the flint and the lamp re-lighted. He played the glaring light on Freeman. No, sir, he realized exultantly, he was still alive!

Keeley found the spotted main fuse and knelt by it. He held the candle to it and the threads glowed; then the powder spat at him like a cat. He dropped the candle and jumped away. Something hit the back of his knees like a sack of grain and he pitched forward.

A stone jarred the gunman's cheekbone, momentarily stunning him. Then he felt the other's fists landing on his back and head, and he crawled to his knees and cuffed him with his fist. Freeman fell aside. Keeley forgot his Colt and simply picked up the lamp and sprang up the slope. The fuse sizzled like an overcharged soda-water bottle. He tripped and fell, and yelled aloud when Freeman caught him about the waist. Keeley struck him, but he clung. He waded up the slope a few feet, stopped and hammered the heel of his fist into the bloody face. Freeman's arms tightened. Panicky, Keeley reached the tunnel and struggled to shake loose, while he moved at a clumsy trot toward the shaft. The mine-lamp sprayed its light this way, that way, over damp rock-facings, and still the lean arms clung. Suddenly they loosened and slid down to his knees. As Keeley sprawled, the lamp clanged on a rock and went out with a brief hissing of gas through a tear in its reservoir.

"*Oh, my God!*" Keeley babbled.

He tore himself away from Freeman, swung at him in the blackness and missed. He began running. The sidewall slammed into his face and he went down. As he got up he imagined he heard the fuse, sizzling like hot fat. For an instant he stood staring blindly, afraid to take a step. For this was darkness so thick it fluttered against your face like moths; it overwhelmed you, murdered your self-confidence, made you want to get down and creep along like a gopher.

But you had only five minutes to get out of here. You had to run for that ladder. And he ran, with long strides, swerving blindly from side-wall to side-wall, crashed down, scrambled up, screaming at the blackness as though he could split it open. Once he thought he heard Freeman's voice, and halted to listen. Then he ran on. Suddenly he smelled smoke— powder-smoke, it seemed. He slowed, tripped, fell to his knees; and as he waited for the strength to rise, he saw an angry spurt of light ahead of him and a little below. Yellow-white, it burned in blackness, illuminating nothing. It must be very far away, he thought, or very small, and he wondered whether he had come to the edge of another pit Haines had forgotten to tell him about. Then he knew what had happened. He had got around turned and come back.

23

"IF THIS IS ALL WE'VE GOT," Tom Haines decided, "it'll have to do. Pick it up, boys."

While Dennis and Galloway shouldered the timber, Haines drew his watch and glanced at it. Eleven minutes had passed . . . Keeley was behind schedule. Just then the ground gave a single tremor. He stared at Dennis, scowling under the weight of the eight-by-eight. A stifled roar blew out of the mine, dust scurried along the ground and loose rocks came rattling down the hillside.

A moment later there was a vibration underfoot—a sort of crumpling sensation. Dennis and the other miner got rid of the timber.

"My God, it's a misfire!" Dennis shouted.

They all ran for the tunnel stopping there to procure lamps from the rack by the adit. "Wait a minute," Dennis panted. "The fumes will poison us. Get out your bandannas—water-barrel's over here—"

Coming back, as they tried to fix wet handkerchiefs over their noses, Haines asked nervously: "Do we dare go in, Charlie? He can't be alive in there."

Dennis looked at him. "When there's a misfire, you go in anyway."

"How long will it be till it clears some?"

"An hour, more or less."

But when they reached the tunnel, Galloway exclaimed: "We've got a draft! Look at that stuff pour out!"

"Probably the tunnel caved in beyond the winze," Dennis speculated, "and this'n's the chimney now. No, wait! It wouldn't come out like that unless there was a shaft coming up from below to give it a draft."

Dennis lighted a lamp and handed it to Haines, lighted another for himself, and the three of them entered the mine. The nauseating fumes settled sulphurously on their tongues.

"There it is," Dennis said, in awe, halting at the edge of the excavation. "Well, you got your glory-hole, all right. And Freeman got his miner's grave. What happened here after we left?"

He turned his head. But Haines was spraying his light over the broken walls below them. "Charlie, what the hell *is* this?" he gasped. "Is there a bottom to that damned stope?"

Dennis looked into the hole again. Dust swirled in the lamp-beams. A damp breeze touched their faces. From their feet the ground dropped away in a long, gray slide. They could not see the far side of the pit at all. At the bottom of the hole was an area of pure darkness, that caused Haines abruptly to move back. Dennis ventured a few feet down the rock-slide. Suddenly he called up:

"There's timbers down there!"

Now there was a roar of moving earth. Terrified, Haines stared across the excavation. Though he could hear it sliding and see its dust rising, he could not see the earth which made the noise. Dennis came scrambling back. "Let's get out of here!"

In the sunlight, Dennis sat on a crate and caught his breath. Then he looked up at Tom Haines, his face grotesquely white where the bandanna had kept the gray dust from it. All at once he was laughing.

"Your Sweet Betsy's gone back to Pike, Haines. Hell, she never left Pike! What you bought was an eggshell."

"What's the joke?" Knowing, somehow, it was no joke, Haines regarded the superintendent gravely.

"This is why Bill Croft couldn't make up his mind. He knew the mountain had already been mined. They must have tunneled into it during the boom, when the ranchers wouldn't let them prospect it. Scooped the ore up and took it out the tunnels a mile away!"

Haines was shaken now, host to a cold vacancy in his belly, but his gambling instinct supported him—the fine art of bluff. He snorted: "Because you saw a couple of timbers in a stope? It must have been prospected before Freeman found it. We just broke into a test-shaft."

"Maybe. But it sounded to me like that test-shaft was about five hundred feet deep."

Teamsters and workmen had quietly assembled about them. Dennis spoke sharply. "Stir yourselves! Get some tools and timbers. We'll take a good look before we give up. Mr. Freeman was in there when the blast went off. Coombs, ride down to the village and send everybody up here."

Haines stayed outside, alone in the sunlight. *So now I own it all,* he reflected; *but what I own is trash.* Quite soon, it seemed to him, a wagon-load of miners arrived from Hornitos. A workman coming out for fresh air told them:

"Wet your handkerchiefs before you go in. It's thicker'n a brush-fire in there."

"We heard the blast broke into an old mine," someone said.

"That's how it looks. We hit the biggest damned glory-hole you ever saw. There's three tunnels leading off it. Maybe more still that're blocked."

Haines walked to the corrals and saddled a horse. He had hoped to get to Brickwood before word of the disaster came to Travertine. But it was too late. So he'd have to cut him in if he wanted to help in doing business with Virgil Croft.

Which he now knew he must and would do. It was all he had left. *All!* he thought. It was still the biggest mining development in a century. And as he rode, Freeman and his Sweet Betsy faded in his mind like the memory of a pot lost in last year's poker game. All he had lost was a single hand—not the game. The twenty-dollar chips were in the pot, now, and the only cards he had to beat were held by an old lunatic across the border.

Until a few moments before the blast Shep was not fully aware of what was taking place. He knew he had to hang onto Keeley, but the gunman's final blow dropped him stunned. Finally he got onto all fours, remembering dazedly the attack by Haines—then the appearance of Johnny Keeley.

A flashing roar like hell burst open knocked him down. There was an eye-aching light, a furnace-blast of heat, an avalanche of sound which crushed him; and then numbness. In the blackness he felt himself moving. It was like lying on a blanket and being pulled over the ground, but the movement grew rougher and faster, until it was more like falling. He rolled and sprawled through a grinding darkness. Then it stopped.

Now is was the silence which impressed him—the utter absence of sound, which in some way was entangled with the lack of light. Lying on his back, he felt blood running from his nostrils. His face was scorched and he could smell burned hair. He put out an arm, testingly. The movement started a small cascade of loose rock. Without rising, he fished matches from his pocket and struck one.

"Where the hell am I?" he muttered in shock. He lay on a slide which choked an old tunnel. The timbers he could see looked black with rot. Inching down to the floor, he moved along a few feet and turned back. Then he understood. The blast had knocked out the bottom of the pit, and beneath it was an ancient system of tunnels, perhaps Spanish or Indian. He had ridden the slide down and had the good luck to stay on top.

With sudden clarity he saw what was likely to happen: the old stulls and timbers would crumble, and another section of this tunnel would collapse. He started at a weaving lope along the drift. When the match went out he struck another and ran on until it died. Behind him he heard a soft *crump* of falling earth. He had a few more matches, and used one to locate a mine-timber which appeared dry. Wedging the match into a cleft, he used his clasp-knife to pull off some long splinters. He got one burning well and started down the drift. Somewhere he would find an outlet. But he couldn't wait for them to cave the tunnel in on him in a rescue operation. Or for honest Tom Haines or Johnny Keeley to find him first and turn rescue into a successful accident.

Several hundred feet along, the tunnel ended and an inclined shaft ran down to a deep level. He scrambled gingerly down it. He was sure, now, that this was a relatively modern mine. A sheet-metal door in a side-wall halted him. Scaling red letters spelled: DANGER! EXPLOSIVES!

He opened the door and looked inside. Except for trash, it was empty. He gazed around. On the floor were some old newspapers. Twisting one into a torch, he lighted it and read the headline of another:

HOLOCAUST IN A BROOKLYN THEATER. 295 DIE IN THE TERRIBLE BLAZE.

December 5, 1876.

He gathered the papers together for torches and started on. Twenty years ago, he thought—boom days in Hornitos. Papers of similar vintage littered the Cloverleaf Saloon. *I own a burned-out mine,* he realized. *I am the proprietor of a dead stope.* And it did not matter, now. His ambition was simply to be the last living miner out of that dead mine. It was a tall and improbable hope, for the drifts might meander for miles, and end in cave-ins and black water.

Dru, Dru, he thought wearily, *you really meant it about your tommyknockers getting down on me.*

The day-coach was parked on a siding while materials for the mine were loaded onto flat-cars, when the hand car from Hornitos arrived. It was hot and dusty in the car. The flies buzzed. Dru fanned herself with a newspaper while she watched four men leap from the hand-car and run for the street. The station-master ran out to ask what the excitement was, and Tom Haines—coatless, she hadn't recognized him—paused to bawl:

"Hold those flats and get up steam! There's been a cave-in. We'll be going right back.''

The girl dropped the newspaper to the floor. A door in her heart opened with a terrible pang—the door she had quietly and positively locked an hour before. When she knew Jessie Haines was going to have him, then, knowing he was not for her anyway, she closed the door of the room in which girls kept those foolish hope-chests of impossible loves.

It went on in her mind while her lip began to tremble. *If you wanted him, why didn't you say so frankly? But girls couldn't do that. Yet it might have helped persuade him to take his money and quit the game. If he loved you, too. I think he did. I felt it. Maybe kissing is always like that—weakness and effervescence and joy. No, it couldn't be like that unless he loved you.*

Men were running down the street and crowding into the car. A man pushed onto the seat beside her. So many times she had seen this play. She knew everything the miners would say, the questions they would ask each other. She remembered that horrible day and night when they were digging for her father.

Oh, if you're going to be dead, be dead when I get there! she pleaded.

Someone shouted: ''Move back, will you! There's a lady trying to get on!''

Dru kept staring out the window. The car was rolling forward at last. The man beside her moved away, and someone touched her shoulder. ''May I sit by you?''

It was Jessie Haines. Dru nodded. The miners kept glancing at them sitting side by side as the train moved into the foothills, as if perhaps they knew about things. Jessie was wadding a handkerchief in her hands. ''Do you know what happened?'' she asked.

''A cave-in.''

''They blasted into an old mine. I guess that's why your father was sort of lukewarm about it.''

''You mean the hill's already been mined?''

''That's what Tom said it looked like.''

''It's too bad. All the men out of work again, and your

investment lost.''

"Oh—Tom and I will get by. Always have,'' Jessie replied.

The tone made Dru look at her. It was a parrot's inflection—no feeling at all. "Why are you going up?'' she asked. "It's the wrong place to wait.''

"Why are you going up? Do you mean you aren't going to wait at the mine?''

Dru looked out the window. "No,'' she said at last. "I'm not going to wait. I'm going to look for him. If they haven't already found him.''

"Look for him! How? The tunnels are blocked.''

"I'm going to the nearest of the old mines and start in one of the tunnels. Probably they're already doing it.''

Jessie smiled wearily. "I thought you Cornish girls never went in the mines, for fear of offending the little people.''

Cinders and smoke blew in the window as the train took a turn. Dru closed her eyes. "What little people?'' she asked.

"Do you mind if we stay together?'' Jessie asked when they left the railroad station at Hornitos.

Dru was walking quickly. "Not if you can keep up.''

"Where is this old mine?''

"Close to the road.''

At the house, she ran in to get one of her father's mine-lamps. On second thought, she took another for Jessie and some extra carbide. A quarter-mile up the road the girls overtook Bill Croft, stumping along with a pry-bar over his shoulder. Dru paused beside him. Jessie was breathing hard and had opened the top buttons of her dress.

"Any news, Dad?'' Dru asked.

Red-faced and sober, her father said: "Not a scrap. The whole thing's caved in like an anthill.''

"Why did you tell Haines the mine was all right?''

Croft stole a glance at Jessie. "Far as I knew, it was. Oh, I knew they'd burrowed around in that general area a bit, but I didn't know how far they went.''

"You worked in the Tiger Tail mine, didn't you? That

must be where they sneaked in from.''

"Yes, but—Well, I thought Haines could gamble on it—''

"At least you must remember the drifts?''

Croft mopped his sweating face with a red bandanna. "Do you remember the trails you had through the brush when you were a kid? The Tiger Tail's twenty years behind me. I remember we started in Number Six drift. I hope to pick it up as I go along. Where are you going?'' he called, as she hurried on.

"To the mine!''

She knew the Tiger Tail mine from playing about it as a child, despite parental warnings. Its grayed gallows-frames, chutes and bins littering the south slope of a mountain were familiar. The huge rock-slides were partially hidden by brush. They searched until they found a tunnel with a cracked sign nailed to the stull: 6. Jessie peered in fearfully at a dark shine of water. There was croaking of frogs. She took the mine-lamp Dru handed her.

"Are—are you sure—?''

"I'm not sure of anything except that he may need us.''

"But it might be better if we waited for your father.''

Dru looked at her. Then she pinned up her skirts and went into the tunnel. Jessie followed. The water was shallow, but littered with debris and stones so that they got through it with almost dry feet. *A half-mile of this!* Dru thought. A half-mile by road, perhaps a couple of miles by the twisting tunnels. With an uneasy stab of guilt, she reflected on the disapproval of the tommyknockers—if by any chance there were such beings—at her invading their inner sanctum. Something flopped from a ledge into the water behind them. Jessie screamed and dropped her lamp.

"It's just a frog!'' Dru told her, her own heart pounding. She found and relighted the lamp. Jessie accepted it. After ten minutes the drift ended. A ladder led upward. Dru tested with the lamp.

"It just goes up a few feet.''

They climbed to a new tunnel and groped along through a few hundred feet of turns. "I've got to rest,'' Jessie gasped.

They stopped. The darkness and silence seemed almost tangible. Suddenly Jessie exclaimed: "Dru, he just can't be alive! Under all this rock?"

"Don't say that! My father was buried for eighteen hours, and *he's alive*."

"With one leg," Jessie murmured. "There's no use going on. What if we do find him? We'll never find our way back."

Would it matter? Dru thought. *If I found him, I wouldn't ask much more.* "Why don't you wait right here until you've rested?" she suggested. "I'll mark all the turns, where there's a choice."

Jessie looked away. "All right." Dru had not gone far when she heard her going back. She felt suddenly terribly alone—alone in a dark and silent world. No: That wasn't true. There were two of them, and they would find each other.

24

TOM HAINES LOOKED AT THE MAP on his office wall, studded with colored pins. Each pin a defunct mine, bankrupt stamp-mill, worthless mineral lease. Sitting with his boots on his desk, he noted the condition of the wine-colored leather scuffed and dusty from the mine. With a brush from a drawer he buffed the toes and finished the job with a dustcloth.

When he left here they'd all be waiting for a look at him. "How had the mighty fallen—"; "Here today, gone tomorrow—" all the smug catch-phrases of the mediocre. The hell with this town he had liked; it had died, though it did not yet know it, when the Sweet Betsy died. *After I settle with the mad metallurgist of Tintown, I won't even have silver around me again—not in my teeth, my pockets; nowhere.* Gold was the charm. You couldn't match gold. Silver was just the ladder he had used to reach the gold.

He walked out and closed the door. A dozen men and women who had been watching now turned away. He smiled coolly. In the late afternoon he walked to the bank—his fourth trip there this afternoon. Brickwood had either had a seizure, or he was hiding from him. There was a self-conscious silence as he entered. He stopped at the chief teller's wicket.

"Oh—hello, Mr. Haines!" the man said. "Any word?"

"Not a word. Is the big chief back yet?" he smiled.

"No, sir. Sent word he'd had to go up to Tucson."

"Give me a couple of counter checks, then." He wrote two checks and pushed one through the wicket. "This is for ten thousand—the balance of the mine account. I'll take goldbacks. Now this other is for five—I hoped to get Carl's okay on it as an overdraft. But don't worry. I spoke to him—All right, dammit!" he said, as the teller began shaking his head. "Make it a personal loan."

Fumbling with a paper cuff, the teller said, "Mr. Brickwood left instructions not to honor any checks over a hundred dollars. I can't cash either of them, Mr. Haines. He wants the week-end to—"

Haines's hand seized the teller's alpaca jacket. "And I want the cash! God damn him, I'll see him in prison if he refuses payment."

The teller looked down at his hand. "I don't want to have to call the marshal, Mr. Haines."

"By heaven, if I don't settle with him!" shouted Haines. He was thinking, *I've given Croft ten already...the ten I forfeit if I don't produce the other fifteen today. What do you do when a bank locks you out? Dynamite it open?*

He tore the checks and threw them in the teller's face. Then he went back to the office. He locked the front door, drew the shades, and looked at the clock. Five o'clock. Three hours till dark. Taking an envelope from his desk, he addressed it to Virgil Croft. Then he took some stock certificates and cut them to the shape of banknotes, stuffed the envelope and sealed it. He took a bar of red sealing wax from his desk, melted a hot, glistening puddle onto the flap and pressed a half-dollar into the wax as a signet.

At last he sat back, to smile at the heavy richness of the envelope. *You said cash, didn't you, Mr. Croft? Yes, sir— right here! Count it.* From the spring clip under his arm he took his small, heavy house-pistol. He loaded five chambers and left the sixth empty where the hammer rested.

In some mines where Shep had worked they posted maps

with a mark to show where you were standing. But this mine had been worked as if by gophers—hastily and not very thoroughly. A drift ended in a blank wall and he had to come back to an X-cut or a ladder to go any farther. But always by some sense his medical texts did not recognize, he knew he was bearing generally northeast. That would be toward the old mine just off the telegraph road. When he was tired, he rested. His watch, still running, said three-twenty. He was hungry, his burned face and hands pained him. Eventually, if he did not find an adit, they would break in and follow him. He had left marks so they could follow each turn he made.

He found another powder-magazine and replenished his supply of newspapers. Old mines were always full of papers. The miners brought their lunches in them, read them, finally gave them decent burial in six-foot holes with powder wrapped in them. He lighted a new torch from the splinter he had been using and stepped back into the drift. Far down the tunnel then, he saw a white, dipping moth of light.

He halted, at first delighted when he saw it move, then wary. He drew the Colt he had never lost. He started to back into the powder magazine when he heard a cry: "Shep! Shep!" He started running, and the cry came again, louder, and he shouted back: "Yes!"

The light stopped moving, but he trotted on until he found the girl standing there. It was Dru. In a moment she came toward him, and he saw that she was weeping. He caught her. "Well, girl! You really fell off the wagon, for your first trip into a mine."

She buried her face against his neck. She kissed his throat, then turned her face away as though ashamed, but still clinging.

"Where are we?" Shep asked her. "Where did you get in?"

"That old mine near the road," she said. "Dad told me about it—they worked this whole area from there."

"You don't mean you came alone?"

"I had someone with me for a while. We got separated."

"I hope you can find the way back," he said. "Did you

mark it?''

"Most of the way. I think I—I'll know the turns, all right.''

"We'd better start,'' he said, and, smiling: "I don't want to keep you out after dark.''

"Dark! There's no darkness in the world, except for miners. I'm glad your mine is dead. Now you aren't chained to it any more.''

They started back. She had marked the main turns, she said, but by four o'clock she was saying faintly that she thought they might have missed one. They worked back to a crosscut and tried a different tunnel. When this one ended in a large, cavelike chamber, they tried another. But this wandered like a tired child's path, and at last, stopping where a new aisle took off to the right, she said faintly:

"We're lost.''

He looked at his watch. "Five o'clock . . . will they wait supper on you?''

She tried to laugh, but it caught in her throat. "I'm that tired I could drop,'' she apologized.

"Stay here, then, while I take a look down this one.''

"I wish I could send the blessing of the little people with you,'' she smiled wanly. "But I think they've gone back to Cornwall.''

Around the second turn he felt a draft on his face. He could almost feel the daylight on his skin as he ran ahead. The sheet-metal door of a powder-room, fallen from its hinges, half-blocked the tunnel. A hundred feet farther he saw the gray beginning of daylight past a turn. He stopped to lean against a timber, closed his eyes and let gratitude run through him like a song. Then he started back for Dru, wanting to be with her when they saw the sun again.

As he passed the powder-magazine a thought came to him. He shot the lamp-beam over the metal skin of the door, which was propped at a steep angle against the wall. He walked back and hung his watch by the fob from a nailhead in the door, so that it rested upon the sheet-metal. It was a cheap watch with a noisy but dependable movement. Magnified by the metal sounding-board, the ticking of the escapement was louder than that of an alarm clock. He smiled with pleasure and went back to Dru.

"We're out!" he said. "The strangest thing happened . . . don't they say you can hear the tommyknockers tightening the stulls and timbers at night?"

She patted his arm as they walked. "You don't have to save my feelings. They were nice to believe in, like Santa Claus. But did they help me when I needed them? I never heard a tap."

"I wonder—" Shep said. "Just now, when I'd gone about so far in this last drift, I decided it was another blind alley. But when I stopped walking, I heard this tapping."

"Tapping!" she said.

"Like hammers or something. Listen!" They stopped, but he shook his head, "I don't hear it, now. Well—maybe it was just settling noises. . . ."

A moment later Dru caught his arm. "Shep, listen! Is that the sound?"

He turned his head. "That's it! It got louder and louder, and suddenly stopped."

As they hurried on, the tapping strengthened. Shep whispered: "I'm going to know for sure this time!" He ran ahead. Dru came close behind. He reached the door and pocketed the watch. He was staring into the empty powder-magazine when she arrived. "There was something, I'll swear—! Like a shadow—no bigger than a small child."

She ventured into the room. "There's nothing now."

"But you heard it yourself."

"Yes. It—it must have been—"

"We'll never know," he decided. "But at least it kept me coming this way." And as they walked on he saw a wondering smile on her lips.

Merry Christmas, he thought. *I took it away from you, but now I've given it back.*

25

WHEN IT WAS DARK, Tom Haines let himself out the rear door of the office. He walked up the alley to the side street and went home. There were lights in the house and he did not go in, not wanting to see Jessie, nor to be seen. He saddled the buckskin and rode a mile west before he crossed the border. The desert darkness was big and warm, with insects chittering in the brush. By side-trails he reached the wash beyond which was Virgil Croft's shack. He tied the horse under the bank and walked quietly down through the wash and up the other side until he came to the adobe house.

He moved carefully about until he could see the old man sitting at the table eating, his bantam rooster perched on the extra chair. He smelled fried meat. A long-barreled rifle lay across the table. Haines decided it must be done boldly. He did not want to kill him, and boldness was the best way to avoid trouble.

"Mr. Croft! It's Tom Haines," he called.

The light went out almost instantly and Haines jumped aside. Something moved behind the unglazed window. "Haines? Where are you?"

"I'm right here. My Lord, did you think it was a thief? I've got the rest of your money."

"Why didn't you come by daylight?"

"I didn't want to be seen. Is everything ready?"

The lamp went on again and the door was unbolted. Haines went into the gloomy cell of the cabin. The bespectacled chemist, rifle in hands, peered at him. Haines glanced at the table, at the shelf behind Croft's rumpled cot, and saw no box, no fitting receptacle for a chemical sample, no long envelope to contain written formulae.

"Where's the money?" growled Croft.

"Where's the formula?" countered Haines.

"You'll see it when I see the color of your money."

Haines sighed and tossed the thick envelope on the table. The rooster cocked his head at it. "Ah-ah!" he exclaimed, as Croft headed for it. "Sweeten the kitty, old-timer."

Croft picked up the envelope and tore it open. "Not till I—" He stared at the stock certificates, then looked up, while his goggling eyes dropped to the small revolver in Haine's hand.

"I'm sorry," Haines said quietly. "I couldn't raise the cash in time. I still mean to pay, but I can't hold to the terms of our bargain. I'm in a bind, and I'll need a little time."

Croft contemptuously threw the papers on the floor. He sat down, picked up his knife and fork, and said to his rooster: "The trash that busts in on you these days, Chucho."

Haines went nearer. "But I mean to have the formula, just the same. Where is it?" He watched Croft's eyes for a careless glance toward the hiding place.

Croft sighed, crossed the room and dug into an open grainsack in a corner. "Chucho, you might as well eat, too."

He returned with a handful of corn and scattered a few grains before the bird. Haines seized his shoulder.

"I won't fool with you!" he warned.

"You better not fool with me," Croft smiled. "Because it ain't wrote down anywhere. And there ain't a teaspoon of chemical in this room, excusing baking soda for my dyspepsy."

Haines hit him with his free hand. Croft covered the cheek he had struck. Haines suddenly strode to the grain-sack and dumped it on the floor. Cracked corn: Nothing else. He stared furiously about the room. Croft was eating again. He gave the rooster some more grain. Haines went to the small wood-stove and looked inside the oven. Slanting a cautious look at Croft now and then, he ripped everything from the shelves back of the stove, the patent medicines from above the bed, threw off the dirty covers and felt of the cornshuck tick.

Panicky, he heard a rustle of movement and turned quickly. Croft was just going out the door. His suspenders flopped at his sides. "Come back here!" Haines said, leveling the gun. The old man yelled—a cackling shriek. Haines fired. Virgil Croft crumpled. The bantam flew to a shelf, squawking.

Haines strode across the room and looked down at Croft. The bullet had entered the back of his head. Blood was spreading from under it, and Haines frowned and gave a shudder. But most of all he was relieved—that he had left town secretly. He felt neither guilt nor pity for this skin-and-bone creature on the floor—irritation, mainly, that he had made it necessary to kill him.

He turned hastily to finish ransacking the cabin. Beneath the cot he could see a small rawhide trunk. But it contained nothing but socks, leather-working tools, some books and at least two dozen tobacco cans. They were all empty. He heard a fluttering sound, a squawk, and looking around he saw that the bantam had flopped to the floor. While he watched, it died. Strange—a seizure of some kind? he wondered. Concussion from the gunshot? But he had no time to wonder about it, and started quickly on a methodical search of the cabin. In a few minutes he was standing in the midst of a litter of clothing, small hardware, overturned sacks and boxes of food, but there was not one scrap of writing, one grain of chemical, to reward him.

He heard a horse run briefly in the night.

He went to the window to listen. He heard it run unevenly, then halt. Uneasily he turned to look once more at the rifled boxes and shelves, the grain spilled over the floor. Some day he would come back, look around for a cache, examine the walls. He started to blow out the lamp, but decided it would be better to leave it burning, as a thief probably would. And then, turning away, he saw the bantam lying near the stove, and was struck again by the strangeness of its death. Suddenly he remember what Croft had said the day he demonstrated his process to them: *"All the gold in Arizona wouldn't bring back your lungs if you breathed them fumes..."*

Poison! By God, maybe he'd had the sample on him—had fed it to the rooster to get rid of it!

Haines took a paring knife from the floor and picked up the bantam, but before he could cut into its craw he heard the horse moving through the brush again, and now he was alarmed. Had Keeley trailed him down here, all the way from Hornitos?

Haines dropped the knife and clutched the bird under his arm. Stepping across Croft's body, he ran from the cabin.

Bill Croft poured two of his cider-and-whisky drinks into Shep, Mrs. Croft kept bringing food, and Dru sat eating little and smiling when he looked up at her. Dennis had come down earlier to say that Johnny Keeley's body had been taken from the mine. But there was still the mystery of why Tom Haines had not returned from Travertine.

Dru walked to the road with Shep when he left. "You still have your cot at the saloon, I suppose?"

"Henry won't be needing it now," Shep guessed. "Neither will I, for long. When I walked out of that tunnel today, I walked out of the mining life forever."

"What kind of life will it be now?" she asked.

"A good one," he said. "Maybe the best. Of course you'll be there to see for yourself."

She smiled, looking very tired but contented. "Of course. Sleep well, Dr. Freeman."

"To dream of Cornish girls," he said.

Before the saloon in the early evening some disconsolate miners were sitting on a bench. Charlie Dennis was having a pipe with them. They looked up at Shep questioningly, and he knew, as a miner, what was in their hearts: *Out of work again, and the bills still to pay.*

"If you'll look in my truck, Dennis," he said, "you'll find a bottle that may help. Personally, I think better times are coming."

"We could do with some. A bachelor like me, now, can always get by. But married men like these—" The other miners gazed at him in astonishment. *"If a man wants to work, he'll find work,"* Dennis used to say. "What makes you think times'll improve?" he asked Shep.

"Have you heard the rumor that there's a new gold-recovery process about to break on us? I've got information that it's true. And when it breaks, boys, they'll be mining glory-holes they abandoned fifty years ago."

"I'll walk down to the station with you," Dennis said. Out of earshot of the others, he asked: "Is that what Bill Croft's been using up here all this time?

"I think so. But they don't have the formula. The pills you threw away that night were some Bill's brother had been giving him. Now it's up for sale. whoever gets it, there'll be jobs for everybody for quite a while."

Dennis helped him set a handcar on the rails. "Where to now?"

"Down the hill. I might as well clean things up with my partner before he leaves town."

"It's my guess he's already left," Dennis confided. "I know a little about that process myself. Haines had a letter from Virgil Croft offering it to him. I don't know whether he ever got it, but when he left here he looked like a man with something on his mind. Maybe he went to close with Croft while he still could."

"To tell you the truth, I've been thinking the same thing."

From Hornitos to Tintown, a man not in a hurry could coast the whole distance. Being in a hurry, Shep leaned on the bar. In a half-hour he jumped off the car at Travertine and walked up the hill to the Sweet Betsy office. The shades were drawn and the door was locked. He crossed the street and went into the Two Nations Saloon. A few lamps burned about the room, and Fletcher Henry was working on a set of books at a table near the bar, his sleeves rolled, his derby on the side of his head, his jaw set.

"Haines been here?" Shep asked him.

"No. But if you see him tell him I'm figuring his bar bill."

Upstreet, Shep found the bank locked and dark. He backed to the edge of the walk and peered up at the office of Haines's lawyer, Jake Lund. No light burned there either, finally he went to a livery stable and rented a saddle-horse.

"Has Mr. Haines taken his horse out this afternoon?" he asked the groom.

"No, sir. I think he walked home."

Through the warm, moonless night he rode to Haines's home. He saw only a light in a bedroom, and as he watched a girl's silhouette passed across the shade. She made several quick trips before the window, like someone packing a trunk. Shep left, convinced she was alone; alone and packing to leave a place which held little of the things she valued— money and position. He did not worry about her: anywhere there were men and money, Jessie would make out.

He had never seen Virgil Croft's place, but in Tintown a man gave him plain instructions for finding it: Down the arroyo a mile to a turnoff to the left; the only house on the east side of the wash was Croft's. A white paring of moon showed above the hills now. Riding slowly, he looked for the turnoff. Far away he heard chickens cackling. At last he saw a light beyond the wash, and turned through the brush toward the cabin. Coming to a low, crumbling bank, he put the horse down it. Across the brush a sound came faintly to him—a flat noise like a door slammed. The horse's ears went forward.

A short distance beyond, he saw movement near the bank, and he drew his Colt and watched. A horse whickered from the spot. His own horse tried to swing toward the sound, but he reined it away. Moving closer finally, he could see that the horse was tied to a root protruding from the bank. He pulled in beside the animal, unbuckled the throat-latch, and threw off the bridle. He gave the horse a whack with his reins and it went crowhopping down the wash. It was the buckskin Keeley had ridden.

He rode slowly over the sand, watching the light in the

cabin. So it was Haines who was transacting business with Croft; Haines, who was always ready to gamble, but getting to like a sure thing too well.

A man was running through the brush from the cabin. Shep swung from the horse and knelt on one knee, the barrel of the Colt lying across his left forearm as he waited. He could see a shape with a wedge of white shirt showing halt on the bank of the wash and study it, and then slide down to the sand and come trotting toward the spot where the horse had been tied. Shep could hear his hard breathing and the crunch of his heels. The man was carrying something under his arm.

"That's far enough," Shep called, and Haines stopped and stared about and finally saw the horse.

"Who is it?" he called.

"An old partner of yours. I got lost in a mine, and look where I came out. Let's go home."

Haines dropped the thing he carried and went for the shoulder-gun, and Shep fired. It drove Haines back. He slipped to his knees. He drew the gun and shot once, the bullet snapping above Shep's head, and Shep fired again. Haines fell onto his side, rested a moment on one elbow and one outstretched hand, and finally slumped face-down. Shep moved toward him cautiously. He took the gun from Haines's hand and slipped it in his pocket. He remembered that Haines had been carrying something, but looking around he found only a dead bantam rooster.

He left it there and rode up to Croft's cabin. Lying in the doorway was an old man who had been shot in the back of the head. The cabin had been ransacked. It was obvious that Haines had tried to acquire by force what perhaps he had been unable to buy. Shep took a blanket from the cot and covered the old man before he left.

He found an empty grain-sack to wrap the rooster in. He did not understand Haines's having taken it, but he was sure Haines must have attached some value to the dead bantam. Perhaps Dru or her father could make sense out of it.

All that made sense to Shep right now was getting back to Dru, and in the warm night, with the moon rising behind him, he rode back to Travertine.